FADE OUT

FADE OUT

nova ren suma

Previously titled *Dani Noir*

SIMON PULSE
New York London Toronto Sydney New Delhi

SIMON PULSE
An imprint of Simon & Schuster Children's Publishing Division
1230 Avenue of the Americas, New York, NY 10020
First Simon Pulse paperback edition July 2012

Previously published as *Dani Noir*.

Also available in an Aladdin hardcover edition.
For information about special discounts for bulk purchases, please contact Simon & Schuster Special Sales at 1-866-506-1949 or business@simonandschuster.com.
The Simon & Schuster Speakers Bureau can bring authors to your live event. For more information or to book an event contact the Simon & Schuster Speakers Bureau at 1-866-248-3049 or visit our website at www.simonspeakers.com.
Designed by Jessica Handelman
The text of this book was set in Venetian 301 BT.
Manufactured in the United States of America
2 4 6 8 10 9 7 5 3 1
The Library of Congress has cataloged the hardcover edition of *Dani Noir* as follows:
Suma, Nova Ren.
Dani noir / by Nova Ren Suma.
p. cm.
Summary: Imaginative thirteen-year-old Dani feels trapped in her small mountain town with only film noir at the local art theater and her depressed mother for company, but while trying to solve a real mystery she learns much about herself and life.
ISBN 978-1-4169-7564-9 (hc)
[1. Motion pictures—Fiction. 2. Mothers and daughters—Fiction. 3. Divorce—Fiction. 4. Remarriage—Fiction. 5. Conduct of life—Fiction. 6. Mystery and detective stories.] I. Title.
PZ7.S95388 Dan 2009 [Fic]—dc22
2009022270
ISBN 978-1-4169-7565-6 (pbk)
ISBN 978-1-4424-5878-9 (eBook)

FOR MOM

AND FOR ERIK,

ALWAYS

CONTENTS

FADE OUT

1

What Would Rita Hayworth Do?

A *slow fade-in on my life:*

There's this little mountain town, smack between two long highways that go nowhere in either direction. There's the one supermarket, the one movie theater, the one Chinese restaurant. But there are twelve different places to buy junk for your lawn.

It's summer, so the days are longer than you can stand. If you want air-conditioning, walk to the convenience store on the corner and take your time searching for an ice pop.

There's this girl. She's thirteen, but if I say she's going on fourteen it might sound better. She's nobody really. You probably wouldn't notice her if I didn't point her out. She's got brown hair to her chin, and bangs that need cutting, and when she reads she has to wear glasses. Today she's got on a tank top that says SUPERSTAR, but that's a big lie so go ahead and ignore it.

She's sitting up on the roof of her house, because that's the only place where she gets cell-phone reception. She checks her phone, finds no messages, not even a text. A truck drives by, doesn't honk. A mosquito sticks its fang in her knee, she smashes it.

Are you asleep yet?

She's me, I'm her. And we're both bored to the gills.

If this were a movie, I would've walked out by now.

So let's cut to black. Roll the credits. Drop the curtain, if this place even has a curtain. Kick the slimy dregs of popcorn under the seat and head home.

Except that would be too soon. Because—just like a movie—there's about to be some big drama when you least expect it. Mine begins when my mom pops her head out the upstairs bathroom window.

Her eyes are puffy—I see this first. Not a good sign.

"Danielle," she calls. "Come inside so we can talk before you go."

"I can't," I say. "I'm sunbathing." Notice I'm flat-out ignoring the fact that she said I'm going anywhere. This is because I'm not. Going, that is. I'm staying right here.

"Sunbathing? It's four thirty in the afternoon and you're in the shade. You haven't even started packing yet. Don't tell me you're out there waiting for Maya to call. . . ."

Maya—she's my best friend. Or she used to be. We met the second day in seventh grade: Fourth-period gym, she held my ankles for sit-ups, I held hers. She was from Willow Elementary and I was from Shanosha Elementary, but soon it was like we'd known each other forever, like her ankles were my ankles and mine were hers. We were inseparable. But ever since she moved an hour-and-a-half away to Poughkeepsie three months ago, she forgot about all that. She's never online anymore and she never calls.

So what if I'm up on the roof waiting for her to call? Or for anyone to call. Even my older brother, Casey, who's away at soccer camp—I wouldn't want to talk to him anyway. If he called maybe I'd pick up and say thanks for leaving me here all by myself to rot, and then I'd hang up on him. But Mom doesn't have to know all that.

"Come inside," she says. "We need to talk."

"Talk to me out here," I say. "I can hear you just fine."

"All right. If you won't come inside . . ."

I wait.

She waits.

The mosquitoes hover.

It's a battle of the wills and I win. It's at this moment that she asks the dumbest question ever: "Dani, do you need help packing your socks?"

Socks! In summer! "Is that what you wanted to talk to me about, really?"

Her voice tightens. "No." But she doesn't say what else it could be. She just says, "You should get packing. Your father's on his way here." Her face gets all crumply as she admits this.

Obviously she's trying to keep from crying. It must be because she just talked to him on the phone. This happens every time he calls: She gets bright pink, her eyes go leaky, and then she holes up in her room.

She's been like this ever since Dad left. Most of the time, like at the newspaper in town where she works, she's a perfectly normal person you wouldn't feel mortified to be seen with. But when she's home with me, she's this other person. She's not my mom anymore but a wobbly pink-headed impostor walking around blowing her nose and pretending she's my mom. I don't know how to act when she's like this. It makes me say things maybe I shouldn't.

Like now. She says, "Come inside, Dani. Please? Your dad's almost here."

And what I could say is *Okay*. I could cut her some slack, you know I should. But instead I say, "And that has to do with me because . . ."

But I'm allowed to be sarcastic. I'm at a "difficult" age, in a "difficult" situation, and you're a liar if you think you wouldn't milk it.

"Because I told you. He's on his way to pick you up right now. You knew this was his weekend. Stop stalling."

This is when the scene goes dark and the music gets loud and, I don't know, thunder crashes in the sky over my head or something. This is when you'd see a close-up of a mouth and hear the scream.

Because I've been telling her and telling her that I'm *not going*. I've told her like twenty million times. I haven't packed a single thing for the trip, and I'm sitting out here on the roof pretending to get a tan but really catching malaria from all the mosquitoes and does this look like I'm going somewhere, does it?

They can't make me go.

Someone will have to drag me kicking and screaming down the driveway, and if the kicking and the screaming don't work, I'll just do one of those nonviolent protests where you play dead so you're as heavy as possible, like a sack of bricks.

I'll make myself like bricks just how Gandhi used to do. At least, I think that was Gandhi, or maybe he was the guy who didn't eat. Anyway, if I have to, I'll pretend to be Gandhi, and who could possibly force me in my dad's car then?

My mom ducks down to grab a tissue. Then her head pops back up, and that's all I see of her, her head, bobbing there like a hot-pink balloon.

She bats her eyes to keep from crying, except all it does is make her nose drip more. She's a wreck. Just listen to her:

"Danielle, you have to go." *Sniffle.* "Even if it's not what *I* want, you know the judge said . . ." *Sniffle.* "I know your dad moved in with that"—she stops herself—"with Cheryl, but that's where he lives now." *Sniffle.* "Dani, can't you understand? You have to go. It's *the law*. . . ." (Here a loud, wet honk as she blows her nose.)

The way she's talking makes me think that what she really wants is for me to *not* pack my socks, to not go.

Then she leaves the window and heads out of sight—I figure to lock herself in her room and soak her pillow. I can make fun of how often my mom cries, but that's because I picked her. In the Cooper-Callanzano divorce of this past winter, let the record show that I chose my mom's side.

Now that my mom has given up, now that no one cares and no one's looking, it gets a little boring out here on the roof. Another truck drives by, doesn't honk. I swat away one last mosquito and climb through the window back into my room.

I take a seat on my bed. My mom put my suitcase there—it's open, empty, waiting for me to shove it full of stuff to take with me. I look at it, and I've lost all the bars on my cell phone, and no one's calling anyway, and I ask myself the only question worth asking:

What would Rita Hayworth do?

Rita Hayworth was this old Hollywood movie star—all glamour and mystery like in those black-and-white movies people like to call "films."

Most of my friends at school have no clue who she is. When they think of a big movie star they think of someone like Reese

Witherspoon. But if Reese and Rita Hayworth were in the same scene and the cameras were rolling you'd forget Reese was even there. And that's not to dis Reese Witherspoon.

All I'm saying is Rita Hayworth was *something*. Say there was this movie and both Rita Hayworth and Reese Witherspoon were in it. Reese would say her lines and she'd be great like usual, but then it would be Rita Hayworth's turn.

Rita Hayworth would toss her hair (red in real life, but in black-and-white it could be any color). She'd blink super slow, like she was underwater. Then she'd turn, finally, and settle her eyes on Reese. It would take a few seconds but feel like forever and you wouldn't be able to stop staring. Then Rita Hayworth would say maybe one word, drawing it out, making it sound like the most beautiful word anyone could say, like, in any language, ever. The word could be "hi" or "mayonnaise," it doesn't matter. And before you know it, Rita Hayworth will have eaten Reese Witherspoon alive.

That's why I think of her. Rita Hayworth wouldn't let anyone push her around, not even Mom and Dad. She'd do what *she* wanted, and no sorrys after.

Rita Hayworth could hide her emotions down where you'd never find them. She'd make you think she didn't care when, really, she cared more than anything. And if someone told her to go someplace—because *it's the law* and *the state of New York says so*—what she'd do is wait till you weren't looking, and then she'd leave for someplace else.

So I decide to make things a little more difficult. Not for myself—for my dad.

Cue the daydream sequence: Dad's car pulls in. He honks from the driveway because he doesn't want to come into the house. He waits and waits and his car's leaking oil and he's all spazzy under the seat belt because he's got that bad back—but I still don't come out of the house. I never come out because I'm not home. It's the first court-ordered visitation and I'm not here to go. That'll show him.

Cut back to real life, and I'm still sitting in my bedroom. Dad hasn't made his way here yet. What I have to do is find a way out before he does.

If this were a movie, I'd jump out the window. A good enough plan, I guess. But if this were an *old* movie—like from the 1940s before all that color, the kind of movie called a "film," one where you'd find someone like Rita Hayworth—I wouldn't even have to jump.

It'd be nighttime, of course, not 4:42 in the afternoon.

There'd be this killer bright light coming in from the window, but in it you'd see only half my face. It's more cinematic that way. My hair's dark—no other word to call it but brown—but in this movie it would be pitch-black. It would shine. And I wouldn't be wearing shorts—I'd have on some long, sparkly dress. Oh—and heels like the spiky ones my mom keeps in the back of her closet even though they hurt her ankles and who knows why she still has them. Plus a hat. I'd have to wear a hat. Back then, girls always wore hats.

The room would be dark and you'd get a tight close-up of just my face. That's when I'd do this whole series of expressions with my eyes.

You'd see fear.

Joy.

Rage.

Bliss.

Misery.

Passion.

Plus lots more stuff I don't even know the words to.

Then I'd take a few steps out of frame and the shadows would swallow me. And no one would be able to find me after that.

But this is no movie and I'm just me, Dani Callanzano, not the kind of name you'd see on a marquee. It's a summer afternoon in upstate New York and I'm thirteen-going-on-fourteen wearing plain shorts and a tank top and sneakers. I've got a cell phone with no bars, an empty suitcase on my bed, and a bug bite on my knee that I can't stop scratching.

So I don't jump out the window. I take the stairs and walk out the back door. I'm not about to let the scene fade out on me—not now, and not without a fight.

And for that, I'd like to thank Rita Hayworth.

2

You Didn't See Me, I'm Not Here

I *head straight for the Little Art movie theater,* the only place worth going to in all of Shanosha, the upstate mountain town where I'm cursed to live.

The Little Art is just like it sounds—it's little, so most of the time people forget it's even there. And it's arty, so when people do remember it's there (like when they park their car in the lot because there's nowhere else to park), they still don't buy a ticket and go in. Hardly anyone does, which is just one more reason to like it, if you ask me.

Right now, the Little Art is showing a "Summer of Noir." In noir movies, there's always some kind of mystery. A bunch of people lie, and you have no idea who's telling the truth. The bad guy isn't always who you think he is—that's one cool thing about noir. Another is that the movies are usually in black-and-white, filled with deep, dark shadows, so if you're looking for somewhere to hide, try inside a movie theater when a film noir is playing.

I'm sneaking down the street when I hear my name. There's a reason most noir films take place at night. You don't see your hero walking around town in broad daylight saying *Hi* and *How's your summer?* to all her neighbors. I knew I should have worn a hat.

Someone calls to me from Taco Juan's, the ice-cream-slash-burrito place across from the Little Art. It's Elissa, my old babysitter. She waves an arm at me through the take-out window. Even though she stopped babysitting me like an eternity ago, I still get to see a lot of her, thanks to her summer job scooping ice cream here in town.

Today she's her usual self—super curly black hair held back so it doesn't get in the hot fudge, a smear of pistachio on her cheek. And her smile, always with that sweet smile, like nothing could ever bring her down. She's really killing my noir mood.

"Dani!" she says, all bubbly. "Want a sundae? On the house!"

Now that she's seen me, I can't just walk away. I give an imperceptible shake of my head, but I guess that isn't enough because Elissa's still talking out the window. "You're not going to see another movie, are you?" she asks. "Wouldn't you rather have some ice cream?"

I stop beside the take-out window, keeping an eye out for any cars passing in the street. "I'm not here," I hiss. "I'm not going to the movies."

She cocks her head, beyond confused. "Okay . . . Then where are you going?"

"To the movies," I explain in a whisper, "except *not*."

Her smile falters for a sec. She blinks. Then she brings out the smile again, even larger this time, and says, "Jimmies and hot fudge?"

Any other day, I'd take the sundae, but this isn't any other day. My world is crashing down around me. Not even ice cream will save me now. Do you hear me, people? This is *serious*.

But I can't stand here and explain this to Elissa. I put a finger to my lips in the universal symbol for "zip it" and just hope, if my mom or dad comes by, that Elissa doesn't crack under the pressure.

What I have to do is get across the street and into that theater before anyone else spots me. I have to—

I turn and crash into a girl who's carrying half the town's public library in her arms. She fumbles but somehow manages to drop only one book. On my foot.

"Sorry, Dani," she says.

I pick it up for her—it's some sparkly-looking book about, wow, is that a unicorn? "What in the world are you reading?" I say.

"Oh, nothing," she says, turning it over so I can't see the cover.

The girl is Taylor. She's in my grade at school. We used to be better friends than we are. If you go way back into the distant reaches of time you'd find Taylor and me, age five or six, getting busted for mixing our Play-Doh in kindergarten. (She had red, I had yellow, we made orange, and BFF from there.) Except, once you hit junior high, you tend to lose sight of Play-Doh.

In junior high what happens is you make a new friend (Maya) and your old friend's still hung up on immature things (like unicorns) and you have absolutely nothing in common anymore, so soon there's no point in even saying hi in the halls.

"So," Taylor says now. "How's your summer?" Her pale blond

hair is up in little braided pigtails that are actually kinda cute. I could compliment her hair, but I don't. Besides, she's in my way.

"My summer's fine," I say. "But if anyone asks, you didn't see me here. Okay?"

"I didn't?"

"Just pretend this whole conversation never happened," I say, taking a step around her. The Little Art is just across the street—so close yet so far away.

"Sorry about Maya," Taylor blurts out.

"Sorry about what about Maya?" I say. "She moved away. She didn't get eaten by a bear." Not a totally ridiculous concept: I once saw a black bear in our backyard. I guess it came down out of the mountains to snack on our garbage or something. This is what I'm dealing with in Shanosha—a town so insignificant the bears don't even bother trying to eat you.

"Uh, yeah, I know she moved away. That's what I meant. But also . . ." She stops.

"Also what?"

"Also about your mom and dad. I wanted to call you, but . . ."

But you didn't.

Taylor just stands there looking at me with this dumb expression, like I'm supposed to respond somehow. She's so caught up in her own world, the one filled with books and whatever you find in them, that sometimes I wonder if she has any idea of what's really happening. Like, in this world. Where we're both standing.

"Gotta go," I say.

I cross the street. Taylor takes the hint and doesn't follow.

But when I reach the Little Art, I'm not free and clear. Ms. Greenway, the theater's owner, is waving at me through the ticket window. She points up to the marquee, raises her eyebrows. That means she thinks I'll appreciate today's movie.

Up on the marquee I see N O T O R I O S in giant letters (as in *Notorious*, directed by Hitchcock—I guess they lost a *U*). That's the movie where Ingrid Bergman is a spy. I give Ms. Greenway the thumbs-up. She knows I like it when the girls get to be spies. I already saw the movie once this week, but I don't mind watching it again. Hey, I'll watch it ten more times if it means not having to go to Dad's this weekend.

I just wish Ms. Greenway never saw me. It's hard to be on the lam from the law—and by that I mean avoiding your mom, who wants you home packing socks—in a small town where everybody and their dog knows who you are.

Before Ms. Greenway can ask me any questions, she gets a

phone call and turns her back to answer it. I take the opportunity to slip inside the theater. I doubt she'd make me pay anyway. We've got what's called an understanding. She looks the other way when I come in flashing yesterday's ticket, she lets me stay for a double feature whenever I want, and she never asks for a thing in return. Okay, so maybe it's not an understanding—maybe she feels sorry for me. Either way, sometimes I think I spend more time at the Little Art than I do my own house.

The lobby of the Little Art is one small room. The walls, floor, and ceiling are all painted black—so you can't see where the walls begin and get tricked into thinking the room's way bigger. There's this velvet rope in front of the theater door even though no one's lined up to wait for the next show. They always keep that velvet rope up—it makes the place seem like a real movie theater.

Only thing is, if you want more toppings on your popcorn in the middle of a movie and you go out to get some, you could trip over the rope and spill popcorn all over the black floor. (In a movie, the camera would push in until all you saw was the dark floor, the pale popcorn. You'd see how spilled white popcorn on black-painted floorboards can sort of look like stars, if you've just fallen over and have the spins and you're sitting there with the mess all around your head. Like a universe of stars. Except you can eat them.)

Maya and I used to come to the Little Art all the time. It was our place. At first we only went to the Little Art because it's across from Taco Juan's, and, you know: free ice cream. Maya wasn't so into the movies here, though. The thing about the Little Art is there's only one movie showing at a time, and it's not always in English. Lots of the movies are in black-and-white and the actors talk really loud and really slow, like they think you need a hearing aid. So I guess it takes some getting used to.

Sometimes when you're watching a movie the reel pops and the screen breaks out in little bubbles that look like boiling black lava's erupting from the moldy ceiling, swallowing the actors' heads. There's dust on the picture, so even the most glamorous of movie stars look like they have dandruff. And sometimes the sound cuts out at the most major scene—like the big reveal when you find out who the masked killer is—so it helps if you can read lips.

What Maya did like about the Little Art was the self-serve popcorn, how you'd scoop it out of the popper yourself and smother it with all different kinds of toppings: salt and butter, sure, but also hot-pepper flakes, cinnamon (my fave), brown sugar, and cocoa powder.

Maya and I would invent new topping combos and snag seats in the second row, which was too close to make much sense of the movie anyway. We'd talk—until some film snob who traveled an hour to see *Citizen Kane* for the fifty-thousandth time told us to shut it. Then we'd whisper. About anything, about everything, about absolutely nothing. It was the best.

Then Maya was gone. But the Little Art was still here.

So I started sitting a little ways back in the theater. That way, my eyes could actually focus on the screen. I started reading the subtitles. I started paying attention.

This is how I first found Rita Hayworth. She was in an old movie called *Gilda*. The first part of the movie is a snore—just these guys in suits talking at each other and you're like yeah-yeah-yeah let's get to Gilda. And then you see her. You *see* her. And nothing is the same after that.

Obviously, Rita Hayworth plays Gilda. There's this part where she has a guitar and she sings in this big room where no one's watching. She's sad, but she's not out-of-control sobbing. She's not pawing through crate-loads of tissues whining, *Why me?*

Then she stops being sad and gets mad. She stands up and throws the guitar and breaks a window. I love that part.

I don't like what comes later so much, when she ends up with the mean guy who used to be her boyfriend and all's forgotten. I like it when she doesn't care what anyone thinks, when she might walk out of the room and never come back, and you know you'd miss her forever. That's the Rita Hayworth I like to remember.

Gilda is what's called a femme fatale. That means she's dangerous. She draws men in, and then she pushes them away, because they can't have her. No one is sure if they can trust her, probably because they can't. The men love her, but they also despise her. They want to know her, and they never ever can. It's complicated, people tell me, like I can't understand the huge messes adults make of their relationships.

But I do understand.

I understand how—in the movies—you walk away at the end knowing who the bad guy is. It's not like in real life when you walk around all confused, wondering if you're the bad one for hating them.

So here I am in the lobby of the Little Art about to sneak into Theater 1 (the *only* theater in the building, so it's kind of funny they bothered with the number)—except someone stops me.

Austin Greenway—Ms. Greenway's son—won't let me in. He holds the velvet rope so high I'd have to be a triathlete to jump over it. But I could just duck under it, and I do. Then he blocks the door. Austin is my age—he'll be in my same eighth-grade class in September. That does not mean I have to be friends with him.

He takes his so-called usher job really seriously—even though he's too young to work legally in the state of New York, so it's not like he's getting paid.

"My mom said if people miss the first fifteen minutes of a show they have to wait for the next one," he says. "And it's been way more than fifteen minutes."

"She doesn't mean *me*, and you know it." I try to stare him down, but he has this way of never meeting my eyes like he doesn't want me to see him. Fine by me.

I mean, he's not beastly or anything—he looks like a normal guy my age. He's normal height. Normal brown hair, normal amount of freckles. Has normal eyes, green I guess, I don't really pay attention. Wears normal T-shirts, normal cargo shorts, normal shoes, if you count man-sandals as normal. Some guys go off for the summer and come back cute—I've seen it happen.

And for a millisecond I think maybe he could be cute if you tilt your head sideways and squint, not that I'm going to try.

"Also, you have to show me your ticket if you want to get in," Austin says.

Strike that. Austin could be cute—but only if he stopped bossing people around. Ever since his mom let him help out at the theater, he's been on a power trip.

"So if I show you my ticket you'll let me in?" I say. "Even though it's been more than fifteen minutes?"

"Do you have a ticket or not, Dani?"

"I have *a* ticket," I say, seeing as I do—technically—have a ticket stub somewhere in my shorts pocket from earlier in the week. I dig in, find it (also an M&M, a blue one, which I count as good luck), and hand it over. Not the M&M, the ticket. The M&M I pop in my mouth and eat.

Austin eyes the ticket up and down. Turns it over. Inspects it. Holds it to his nose like he's sniffing it for clues. I wish that were a joke.

In the movies there'd really be no place for Austin. He wouldn't be the hero. He wouldn't be the bad guy either. He wouldn't even be the funny sidekick, because I'm looking at Austin right now and I'm so not laughing.

I guess he could be a minor character—an extra. Sure, that's what he'd be, an extra, like the guy who holds the door open for Rita Hayworth as she sweeps into the nightclub. If he's lucky he has one line like, "Good evening," or "May I take your coat?" He's so insignificant, he doesn't even get a name in the credits. His character is called Guy Who Took Rita Hayworth's Coat. That's the best I can do for Austin.

Not that I'm Rita Hayworth in this scenario or anything. Still, would it kill him to open the door to Theater 1 and let me in?

Guess so. Because here's Austin, still eyeing my ticket.

Maybe the Little Art should be better about their ticketing system, because the ink doesn't always work on the machine and my old ticket looks like any other ticket—you can't tell what show it's for. My ticket is the color of a ticket. The shape of a ticket. For all intents and purposes, a ticket. And Austin knows it. Which makes me grin.

"You saw this show already," he says at last, "on Wednesday, the four fifteen, remember? *Notorious*? By Hitchcock? With Cary Grant and Ingrid Bergman? I remember seeing you. I know you were there."

"So?"

"You're just here to bother Jackson, aren't you?"

Things about Austin:

(1) He's way annoying, can't mention that enough.

And (2) he's obsessed with his cousin Jackson.

Jackson works here for the summer as a projectionist. That's the person who sits up in the booth at the far back of the theater. You know that little window up above the last row of seats? The window where the movie comes out of? At the Little Art, there's an actual human someone in there, making it happen.

Jackson's seventeen—the same age as my old babysitter, Elissa. He's in high school, and he says he's working here only to save enough money for a car. He talks about the car a lot, but we also talk about movies sometimes, about Rita Hayworth. Austin hates it—Jackson never asks *him* who his favorite femme fatale is.

When Jackson's with me, it's different. I can't even talk about it with anyone. I mean, I know nothing could happen. I'm not dim. I know how far the divide is between high school and middle school, like between black-and-white and full-color, between silver screen and squeaky movie theater seat in the audience of real life.

Besides, Jackson has a girlfriend. And not just any girlfriend:

Elissa. And Elissa's like family. When someone used to put you in pajamas and make you brush your teeth, you can't help but have a deep, unspoken connection. That means any boyfriend of Elissa's is automatically a friend of mine. That's all.

Anyway, what I like about Jackson is how he leaves me alone. He sees that I want to watch a movie and he just lets me watch. He doesn't ask, *How are you* feeling *about the divorce?* He doesn't say, *Why do you spend so much time here? Don't you have any friends?* He'll let me hide here as long as I want to. And that's all I care about today.

But back to Austin. Because he's standing here, still blocking the door to Theater 1, like only over his dead body will I get in.

"You *are* going in there to talk to my cousin, aren't you?" he says. He tries to narrow his eyes into sharp points, but it just looks like he got soap in them. "What do you want to talk to him about anyway?"

"None of your business," I say.

"Why won't you admit you're in love with him?"

I did not just hear those words.

Austin doesn't actually think that. The kid has no idea. Which brings me to (3): Really, Austin just hates it that *anyone* would rather talk to me than to him. It's like he can't fathom that I could be more interesting than he is, like that's more unbelievable than the existence of, I don't know, aliens.

(And by the way, I do believe in aliens, it's completely egotistical not to, and I'd bet a trillion dollars that Austin doesn't.)

Austin's still standing in front of the door when his mom calls for him on the walkie. Seriously. Austin's brilliant idea this summer was to use walkie-talkies so his mom could reach him anywhere in the theater. Not that she simply couldn't yell out *Austin!* and he'd hear her and answer—he just happens to be insane.

He holds up a hand to me and says into the walkie, "Austin here."

Ms. Greenway's staticky voice says, "Is Danielle there with you? Tell her that her mother's on the phone."

"Ten-four," Austin says. (It's so much worse when he uses the technical language.) Then he turns to me, all smuglike. "Your mom's on the phone."

"I'm standing right here, Austin. I heard."

He motions at the house phone in the hallway. "So go get the phone."

Which of course I am not about to do. So instead I lean in and I try to be as nice as possible to him, which is like eating ants, and I say, "You didn't see me. I'm like Orson Welles in *The Third Man*. I'm not here."

That's the movie where this guy, played by Orson Welles, spends the whole time sneaking around in dank, dark sewer tunnels under the city. People are looking for him, but he's hiding, just out of sight, being the third man no one can find. That's me—only I don't reek like a sewer. Now, if only Austin will let me in . . .

But he says, "You're like who in what?"

And this is the guy who works at the movie theater.

"Just never mind, okay? If my mom asks, you didn't see me. That's all I meant."

No matter what complaints I've got about Austin, I guess there's also (4) Austin's not so strong. Physically, I mean. I'm able to shove him out of the way, open the door to Theater 1, and walk on in.

3

But Mom's Not Exactly Ingrid Bergman

M*aybe this would be the part of the movie* where we'd go back in time to see how it all happened. That's called a flashback. Like, I open the door to Theater 1, take a step into the darkness, and my whole life spins out before my eyes: being born, first word, first step, that time with Taylor and the Play-Doh, that time on the jungle gym when I almost broke my arm, learning to snowboard up on Hunter Mountain, learning—fine, *failing*—to play bass guitar, first kiss (practice), first kiss (clumsy but real), that time I held Maya's ankles when she did sit-ups, that time she held mine, that time I tripped over my shoelaces outside the school library the first week of seventh grade and fell flat on my face and everyone laughed and I wish I could forget it but I can't, that time my best friend moved away, that time I found out someone was lying and that someone was my dad.

You've got a little time to dwell, in a movie. Right now, not so much. Here I am walking into Theater 1, and yeah, it's dark, but I'm definitely not getting any flashbacks.

What I see is that the film's rolling, which means Jackson's up in the projection booth, as usual. The theater's practically empty. I take a few steps down the aisle. When I look back up at the booth I can see Jackson's shadow through the tiny window, just his head, the film reel spinning slowly beside him. From that window, a bright tunnel of light shoots out at the screen. It's near impossible to look at, like staring straight up at the sun.

I take an aisle seat. The movie's nearing its end—we just found out that Ingrid Bergman is being poisoned by her evil husband and his more evil mother. Cary Grant is there to save her. All this time he wouldn't admit he loved her, but now, just before it's too late, when she's weak and can't stay awake and could die practically any second, he says he does.

"I was a fatheaded guy full of pain," he tells her. Then he takes her away. It's never too late, I guess is what the movie's saying, to say you're sorry you had a fat head.

When the gray title card appears, announcing THE END, I stay put. There are only two other people watching the movie. They sit halfway across the theater from each other—but before the house lights even come on they get up and head for the exit.

While the credits roll, I think about Mom. And Dad. I think about how this is the worst summer, like, *ever*, and I think about the three mosquito bites I've got—no, wait, four—and I think about Maya, and Jackson, and then Austin, which has me thinking about aliens, but that just makes me think about Mom and Dad all over again.

I'm still thinking when the credits end and the lights go on, which is only making things worse, so I stalk up the left-hand aisle to the projection booth and knock on the door on that side. If Jackson lets me hide in there, he can talk about cars all he wants—maybe by the time he's done Dad will have left town without me.

Jackson opens the door a crack. I see one eye—but he won't open the door any farther. He's got sandy-colored hair that's always falling in his face, and he wears these suit jackets with

T-shirts, like he's going somewhere important at the last minute but forgot the whole rest of his suit at home.

"It's not my fault," Jackson says. "The reel got jammed."

"What reel?" I say, confused. "It's me, Dani."

He opens the door a little wider. "Oh hey, D, didn't know it was you."

Jackson's the only one who ever calls me D—I kind of don't mind it. He's the only person alive who could get away with giving me a nickname.

He glances around to make sure the theater's empty. "The reel didn't get stuck," he admits, pushing hair out of his eyes. "I just got distracted and forgot to change it in time. So they had a little intermission, no big. My aunt didn't see, did she?"

"I have no idea. . . . Distracted by what?" The way he's keeping the door open only a minuscule crack of a crack makes it so I can't see for myself.

"Nothin'," he says. "So what's up? You want something?"

"Why do you say that?"

"You knocked."

Oh, right—guess I did.

I shrug, trying to look all casual. But the truth is, I *really* want inside that projection booth. My mom would never think to look for me in there, never. And maybe Jackson would let me in if I just explained what's going on, but I don't know him that well, not like I know his girlfriend, Elissa.

I can tell Elissa anything. She knows all about how my dad left, for example. She knows that my dad was cheating for months before we found out about it. She knows everything, really, and now that Maya's gone I guess she's the only one who does.

I don't know how much Elissa's told Jackson. They haven't been together long—like a month and a half, ever since he moved to town to stay the summer with his aunt. But still, six weeks is a long enough time to spill all my secrets. I'm almost afraid to ask.

Maybe he sees this on my face, because he suddenly steps out of the projection booth, closes the door, and leads me down the aisle toward a seat up front. "Looks like you need to talk," he's saying. "We've got the whole place to ourselves between shows, so you go ahead and talk, I'll listen."

But I don't really want to talk—I want to hide. What, does he think I'll knock over the projector and get shoeprints all up and down *Casablanca* or something?

We sit in the second row, my and Maya's row. Up close and

personal to the screen but still with somewhere to prop our feet. The screen is blank, and the lights are up so we can see the grease stains on the seats. He's right next to me. That's his elbow touching my elbow.

"So?" he says. "This isn't about Rita Hayworth again, is it?"

When I don't answer—and you know you're in a bad mood when you don't want to talk about Rita Hayworth—he shrugs and shifts in his seat so his elbow isn't anywhere near mine, and starts updating me on how much he's saved for his car. He wants the kind of car you'd find in an old movie, the kind with fins and tails, what he calls a classic. If he works at the Little Art all summer, he might be able to save enough so he won't have to keep riding his bike around like a kid. ("No offense," he says, so of course I take offense now.) He's staying at his aunt's for free so he can work all the hours he can get, but the Little Art needs to show more movies. He's got this idea, only Ms. Greenway hasn't said yes yet. "The Midnight Movie," he's saying. "Half-price, Saturday nights. Everyone in town'll be there. What do you think, should my car be blue, black, or, I dunno, red?"

I can't listen to this stuff about the car anymore. I don't know how Elissa stands it. Without warning, I explode: "If you want to know what happened, I'll tell you. I ran away!"

He pauses, then says, "You ran away, huh? . . . That's heavy. But you didn't think to wait till after dinner?"

I have to assume he's teasing. Obviously I plan to be home in time for dinner.

But, you know, now that I think about it, if this were a movie I *would've* run away. Like, with a hobo bag on a stick and everything. And if the cops picked me up—say while I was about to hop the freight train—I'd be in handcuffs on my way to juvie. But in real life I guess you could say I just took a walk.

Jackson leans back in his seat. "You didn't really run away, did you?" he says.

"Not exactly."

"But your mom doesn't know you're here right now, does she?"

"No. But if she asks, I'm like Orson Welles in *The Third Man*, okay?"

"Got it. I didn't see you. You're not here."

I nod. Sometimes there are people who just *get* it. Sometimes these people are going out with your old babysitter because they think you're a kid who rides around on a tricycle, but still.

"So how long have you been missing?" he says with a straight face.

I check the clock on my cell phone—paid for by my dad;

I should pitch it in the garbage—but it's searching for service again. When it gets no signal, it can't even tell the time right. "Maybe a half hour," I say. "I don't know, the stupid thing's broken."

I let the phone drain its battery on the seat next to me. I can't even look at it, this dumb phone my dad got me when he moved out. It's so I can always call him to talk, but the phone barely works unless I'm up on the roof, so what's the point? It's like he got me a phone I can't use on purpose—so he'd never get the call where I up and ask him why he did what he did.

Besides, the phone is pink. *Pink.* A femme fatale would have a sleek black phone with tiny buttons, a thin sliver kept in her hip pocket. She'd set the ringer to silent. And she'd get calls all the time, but she'd rarely answer. What femme fatale would?

"That is one seriously ugly phone," Jackson says, and I cringe—it's not like I picked it. "So why'd you 'run away'?" he says. "What happened?"

"They're making me go to my dad's new place for the weekend."

"Where *is* his new place?"

"Somewhere all the way on the other side of the river."

"What town? You know I'm from—"

"Who cares what town? I have to go for the whole entire weekend. I won't go. They can't make me. I'll stay here. I'll move in to the Little Art if I have to."

Jackson lets this sit between us, this threat I made that we both know I'll never follow through with—I don't have it in me. He stares out at the blank movie screen for the longest time, trying to find the words, or the right moment, or . . . something.

Finally he says, "That's heavy. But you know what, D? Elissa told me what's been going on. Maybe you should give your dad a chance here."

I bolt upright in my seat. "What for? He cheated. He's a cheater. He ruined my mom's life. He ruined *my* life. A chance to do what?!"

"To still be in your life, maybe," Jackson says.

I roll my eyes. I should've figured he knew. I just didn't expect him to say this.

"To be your *dad*," he continues. "Even though he . . . you know . . . he's still your dad."

"He's a cheater!" I burst out again.

"Hey, hey," he says. "Chill. You know how in *Notorious* Ingrid Bergman has to marry that slimeball because she's a spy but really she's in love with Cary Grant?"

"Yeah . . ."

"Life's complicated," he says. It seems like he's going to say something else, but he leaves it at that. He's seventeen, a whole four years wiser than me, and all he can tell me is life is complicated? Yeah, *and*?

Besides, it feels even worse coming from him. Maybe there are some people who don't get you at all. Who never will. Because he was never supposed to. Because he's just some guy who changes reels at a movie theater and that's it.

I feel sick to my stomach. I shouldn't have eaten that grungy M&M.

When Mom found out about Dad, there was this huge fight. Lots of screaming. Dad told Mom he was leaving. He told her he wanted to be with that other woman—he kept saying her name so I couldn't help but hear it. *Cheryl*.

The end between my dad and my mom was obvious. But the end between me and Dad—it's like it never happened. I didn't get to scream at him. He didn't try to explain. After he had that big fight with Mom, he was just gone, out of the house. Like he'd broken up with both of us.

And now he expects me to go stay in this house where he lives with his girlfriend, Cheryl, and her daughter, some girl I've never met. Like he's saying this kind of thing happens all the time and life goes on and *wah-wah-wah* and, here, try some of Cheryl's lasagna on our brand-new dishes.

"So you're not speaking to me now?" Jackson says.

"I'm speaking to you," I say stonily.

"And?"

"Jackson," I say at last, trying so very hard to keep my voice in check, "how is this thing with my mom anything like *Notorious*? My mom isn't Ingrid Bergman. I mean, sure, she's acting weird right now. But she hasn't gone over to the dark side—she's just depressed."

I catch him stealing a glance at the projection booth like he's lost complete and total interest in our conversation. "Hey, speaking of Orson Welles," he says, "there's something you *have* to see. It's this reel we just got, *Touch of Evil*. It's classic. The opening shot is genius. It was done in only one take, so don't blink or you'll miss something."

"Uh, okay . . ." Then he races back to the projection booth. Of course he doesn't care. Why'd I think he would?

The light of the projector comes up—showing only a bright patch of white with specks of dust flying through it. A reverse snowstorm.

I hear a few ominous notes of music. Then I see a close-up of two hands hiding a bomb in the trunk of a car. The person who planted the bomb runs off into the night, and a clueless girl and her clueless boyfriend get in the car like nothing happened.

I watch the car pull away. I watch, and the camera follows. The car pulls onto another dark street, and the camera turns its eye to a new girl and her boyfriend, and when it does, the car cuts the corner and is gone.

Jackson said don't blink, so I don't take my eyes off the screen. I can't help but do what he says, even when I'm steaming mad at him.

I watch the new couple walk down the street, past crowded doorways, past parked cars, past—what's that, a goat? They come to a stop at the border of Mexico and then the car from the beginning pulls up behind them. There's the sound of something ticking, and the car speeds off, and just when the guy on the street leans in to kiss his girl, a loud blast shatters everything. A bomb just went off.

They pull apart, turn to look, and for the first time since the movie started the camera cuts away to—

To . . . ?

To a fuzzy something. A big blur.

"Hey!" I yell over my shoulder. "I can't see what happened!"

Jackson's not answering. I turn around in my seat and look for him in the projection booth. I can see him in there, his head at first, only his head.

Until there's a second head. A second head very close to his head. *Intimately* close, in a way that makes me think I must be seeing things.

He's not kissing someone, no. He's only in there talking, whispering to someone, that's all—but who?

Then I get it. It's Austin, it has to be. That little worm is getting me in trouble.

You know what? I'll be gone before he does. I pop up out of my seat and book it to the exit. I'm out the door and past the red velvet rope in the black-box lobby, where I take a moment to stop and catch my breath. I am *so* going to get Austin.

Only, Austin's standing right here.

"You can't have your money back," he says. "Even if you hate the movie—it's company policy. Besides, you didn't pay so I don't even know why I'm telling you."

"You were just in there spying on me, weren't you?"

"I was not. For your information, I didn't leave my post."

"Okay, okay, but you were in the projection booth, right? Talking to Jackson?"

"Negative."

Not kissing, I tell myself. *Not kissing.* "Austin, just tell the truth."

"Dani," he says, looking utterly lost, "I've been out here the whole time."

I hate to say it, but I believe him. "I guess it was someone else," I say, glancing at the closed theater door.

"Yeah, a girl," Austin says.

I stand stock-still. "What girl?"

He shrugs. "Didn't see who it was. She snuck in when I was, um . . . okay, I left for just a few seconds and I saw her when I was coming out of the bathroom. She didn't pay for her ticket either." He says this last bit with a sharp glare at me, but I ignore it.

"Elissa? Why didn't you say so!"

"Not Elissa. A girl. If it was Elissa, I would have just said Elissa."

"Of course it's Elissa," I say. It's the only possibility that makes sense. Jackson wouldn't have been in there whispering—or doing something more than whispering—with anyone else.

"I'm going to go say hi," I say. But before I can, a high-pitched shriek escapes out Austin's pocket. I jump. He jumps.

Then he looks down at his shorts pocket and says, "It's just the walkie."

It's his mom, Ms. Greenway: "Austin, go find Danielle and tell her that her mother's here."

"Ten-four," Austin says with this huge, obnoxious smile. Then he shoves the walkie-talkie back in his pocket. He looks me straight in the eye and says with what I can tell is great satisfaction: "Hey, Dani, your mom's here."

I could kick him.

My mom storms in, her face hot pink and filled to bursting with helium, but this time it's because she's mad at me. "Danielle! Your father will be at the house any minute! We're leaving. *Now.*"

I'm afraid she'll go all Niagara in front of Austin, so I don't protest.

In a flash I'm at the car while she searches for her keys. She's parked in the no-parking emergency space out in front of Taco Juan's—that's how not-herself she is. Also, she somehow seems to have lost her keys between parking and walking across the street.

"Do you see them?" she mutters. "Did I drop them?" She searches the asphalt all the way out to the yellow line in the middle of the road. The shiny thing she thinks could be her keys turns out to be a crushed soda can—Mountain Dew, I think.

That's when I see someone waving at me from inside Taco Juan's. A head pokes out the take-out window, and that head belongs to Elissa.

My mind buzzes with nothingness as she calls out to me. Something dead-center in my chest tightens into a ball of hurt. For her, I tell myself. Mostly for her. "Hey, Dani! So do you want that sundae or not? Told you, it's on the house."

Slowly, I shake my head. "No, thanks," I hear myself say. I'm still trying to find a way to explain how she made it out of the theater and into the lobby—where I'd been standing—and across the street—where I am now—onto the sidewalk and back inside Taco Juan's without me seeing a thing.

"Dani, you never turn down a free sundae," Elissa says. "Are you okay?"

"Yeah, I'm fine." At least I think I am.

Her eyes widen at the sight of something in the street. "Um, you might want to get your mom out of the road before she's hit by that bus."

I speed over and pull my mom out of the intersection. The

Pine Hill Trailways bus trundles past without running her over. I have to get her out of here. I need to get out of here myself. So I wave thanks to Elissa and lead my mom to our hatchback. It's when we reach the curb that my mom notices the keys in the ignition, windows down. Her face pales, finally. She shrinks back to normal size. "They were here the whole time," she says. "I can't believe they were here the whole time."

As we get in the car, she's having trouble looking at me. "I'm sorry," she says, staring out through a windshield that desperately needs washing. "This is a hard day."

Sarcastic snaps fill my head. They stomp around like elephants, wanting out. But I keep them down and all I say is, "I know."

"And you're not making it any easier," she adds.

Again I say, "I know." I say it, but I guess I don't *know*-know. I have no idea what it feels like to be her right now. She's sitting here next to me, not talking and not driving, and I wish she'd just start the engine and *go*.

She glances across the street, up toward the offices of *The Shanosha Scoop*, the newspaper where she works. It's one block down from the Little Art, just across from Taco Juan's. "Dani, I just remembered that I need to run in and get some work to take home for the weekend," she says. "Can I trust you to stay in this car?"

"Yes," I assure her.

She touches my arm, holds my eyes in hers. "I'm trusting you. I'll be back in a minute."

"You can trust me," I say as she leaves the car. She can trust me, I think to myself as I watch her cross the street. I will stay in this car. I will go to my dad's for the weekend. I will not cause my mom any more trouble.

And I am trustworthy, I am as good as my word . . . until I catch a glimpse of something strange. Something I don't want to see.

The fire door at the side of the Little Art just opened—the emergency exit leading out of the theater and into the parking lot, the one door no one ever uses. Well, someone just came out of that door. A girl.

The fence and parked cars block my view, so at first I think my eyes are playing tricks on me, that I'm seeing spots. But then I realize the girl's just wearing polka dots.

Someone else would go, Huh. There's some girl slipping out the fire door. Maybe she was in the projection booth making out with Jackson. . . . Oh, well, I'll just sit here fiddling with the radio until my mom comes back since it's none of my business, because it's not like he's my boyfriend, and it's not like I care who he kisses in the dark with the door closed.

I am not that someone.

I'm the kind of someone who unsnaps her seat belt and opens the door, even though she promised to stay put. I'm a nosy someone. A determined someone.

I'm the someone who would never forgive herself if she didn't get out of that car and follow the girl.

4

The Femme Fatale, Take One

I *sneak down the sidewalk* and across to the parking lot behind the Little Art. I follow the girl.

All I can see is her back: She has hair to her shoulders—bright burgundy when it catches the sun. She wears a skirt, black. A tank top, black. And oddest of all, footless tights with spots all over them, dark pink and stark white, like she broke out in some sort of heinous rash just on her legs. I figure she's in high school. But I'm guessing—because I can't see her face. Even so, I am positive I have never seen this girl in my life.

She walks across the parking lot and I follow the path of her polka dots. I duck down behind a car as she checks for a rock in her shoe. Then she steps out of the parking lot onto Upper Canyon Road. I wait a few seconds before I go after her. She sticks to the side of the road even though there's no sidewalk. I stay put behind a tree.

I'm thinking about movies again. About one very specific movie, the one playing in my head.

Because if this were a scene in a movie, it would be full of suspense and dodges and near-escapes and your heart would thump in your chest as you watched it, your heart up in your throat as the detective—you know that's me—sneaks down the alley. But the femme fatale keeps turning the corner before you can see who she is.

It would be deep night, the only light from a few sparse streetlamps.

There'd be a whole sea of shadows.

It would start to rain and she'd pull out a black umbrella, pop it open. As she does you'd catch a flash of her hair. A quick shot of her cheek. Then the umbrella would cover her up, making it impossible now to find her face.

You'd hear the sound of her shoes even through the rain. *Clack, clack. Clack, clack. Clack, clack.*

And my shoes too, fainter but still there—if this were a movie I would not be wearing sneakers.

We'd be in a big city nowhere near Shanosha. We'd be where all the movies take place, where things actually happen.

The streets would be cobblestone, not cracked asphalt with weeds bursting through. The buildings would be way taller than two stories. Up in the sky would be the lights of a city, not the lumpy old mountains that don't light up in the night at all.

But, soon enough, the femme fatale would realize she's being followed. She'd lift the umbrella to peek over her shoulder and you'd catch a glimpse of her eyes—dark-painted, narrowed with suspicion, but still calling you closer, drawing you in.

She'd duck down a side passage, and you'd follow. Only, it's a trick, a dead end. You'd find a wall, bricked up, no exits. Somewhere deep in those shadows she'd have to be hiding, but as you stand there in the dark, straining to hear through the rain, you'd swear she got away.

This may not be a movie, but the girl in the polka-dot tights does take a turn somewhere because, peeking out from my spot behind the tree, it looks like I lost her.

Or maybe she got into that car parked all the way up the street—I can't see from here. I have to get closer. I step out from behind the tree and stay low, letting the Fosters' unruly hedge be my cover (I happen to be standing on their lawn). I'm getting ready to make a run for it when my mom finds me.

She's pulled up in the hatchback. "Danielle," she says, "what in the world are you doing? I told you to stay in the car."

"I thought I saw—" I start, then think better of it. Austin might know about the girl, but I shouldn't tell anyone else, not till I'm sure.

"You thought you saw what?" My mom's not going to let me get away with this.

"A kitten," I say. "A little baby kitten."

"Where?" my mom says, looking around wildly. Good choice, Dani. Mom *loves* kittens.

It seems like she may actually get out of the car to search. Then she remembers we have somewhere to be—that my dad will be at the house any minute, if he's not there already—and she makes me get in and put on my seat belt.

"The kitten must belong to someone," she says as we pull off Upper Canyon and back to the main road. "Don't worry," she says as we take the turn to our house, "the kitten will be just fine."

But you and I know there's no kitten. This is all one huge

diversion, see, this part of the movie. Because what's really happening is someone's been lying and breaking hearts, and that's not fiction, that's not a picture on screen. That's real life.

Someone is being a big fatheaded liar like my dad.

And it all has something to do with a girl in polka-dot tights.

5

A Little White Lie

H*ey, you.*

Yeah, you. You in the car with your face smushed against the glass. The one sulking. The one who forgot to pack socks. How's it feel to lose?

I won't dignify my own self with an answer.

My whole rebellion thing went nowhere and fast, there's no denying it. I mean, if I look out the car window I see the tollbooth, which is how I know we're coming up to the Rhinecliff Bridge. Once we cross that, we'll be on the other side of the Hudson River. In Dad's territory. Where I said I wouldn't go.

Dad reaches out an arm to pay the toll. With the window rolled down, the air-conditioning leaks out and the scent of the river seeps in. If you've never crossed the hideous Rhinecliff Bridge heading east on a summer's night when you'd rather be anywhere else, I'll tell you what it smells like:

Mud.

Dad's paid the toll and we're moving again. Soon we'll be on the bridge, and we can't turn around once we're on a bridge, I think that's illegal. I haven't spoken a word to him since we left Shanosha.

I'm sitting in the passenger seat in such a way that I'd have to physically crank my neck all the way around to look at him, but that doesn't mean I can't see him with the eyes in the back of my head. That doesn't mean I'm not aware of every single thing he does as he pulls the car onto the bridge. Like how he puts a little weight on the brake now, like how he keeps glancing at me when he really should be keeping his eyes on the road.

I can't help but notice that he looks the same. Only a couple months have passed, and I guess I figured he'd have changed. Like he'd come pick me up with a beard or something and I'd be like *Who's that dude? That dude's not my dad.* But no. He's here and he sure looks like my dad. He has the short dark hair that sticks up on top, always, no matter if you smooth it down with gel or spit. The same brown glasses, and behind them the same pair of gray-green eyes. Somehow it feels so much worse that he looks exactly like my dad.

I aim my eyes out the window where I can see the edge of the bridge and, below and beyond that, the water. I can see the mountains—the same ones I have by my house—and up above them in the sky, all pretty just to be annoying, the orange-pinkish glow of the setting sun.

Hey, you.

Yeah, you. The one who was in the dark theater getting played. The one dragged out by her mommy. Some Rita Hayworth you turned out to be.

"Did you say something?" Dad says. We're coasting over the bridge now.

I make a great show of adjusting the shoulder strap of my seat belt so I don't die of suffocation. But I don't answer.

"So it's the silent treatment all weekend, then," Dad says. "I thought you were more mature than that, Danielle."

Mature. *He's* talking to *me* about being mature. I let go of the shoulder strap so it cuts into my throat, constricting my air passage, making it impossible for me to speak even if I wanted to. Below us is the water of the Hudson, dull and gray.

Dad says, "Fine. You don't have to talk. I'll do all the talking. This has been . . . difficult, for all of us. And I take the blame for this, Danielle, I want you to know that."

I've been trying to keep absolutely silent, but I lose control for one second and let out a sound: a cross between a snort and *ha!* Like *pfffftcha*, which needs no translation.

Dad keeps talking, being all *You have every right to be mad at me.* Saying *I did some things I'm not proud of* and *I hope you can forgive me.* Adding *Blah-blah I'm your dad and I'll always love you, blah.*

If this were a movie and the heroine's dad was being a major liar like mine, we'd throw in a car chase to get rid of him. Like maybe I'd get so mad, I'd run out to escape him and he'd go after me, do an illegal U-turn on the bridge, speed away from the cops, cause a traffic jam, run over some poor kid's dog, and land in prison.

In real life, what I want to do is tell my dad I'm not dumb. I pay attention. If there's anything I've learned from noir movies it's that everyone lies about something. And if you lie about one thing, what's to say you didn't lie about it all? I'd like to hear his answer to *that*.

Of course, I don't say any of this because I can't: I'm still not talking to him. But I think it. I think it really, really hard and hope he hears me.

When we reach the end of the bridge, the car in front of us turns right and we keep on going straight. I don't know where my dad lives now—except that it's somewhere on this side of the river. I decide to close my eyes so I can't find it, even if I was forced to.

I let the noise of this side of the river wash over me. Car noise, air-conditioner noise, radio noise, all noises we have on my side of the river.

Eventually, the car slows. I feel it turn. A touch of brakes as we come to a stop. We have arrived, I take it. We're at his house. My eyes stay sealed.

"*Danielle,*" I hear him say.

I hear a loud sigh. Then the key being pulled from the ignition, the driver's side door opening.

"Dani, do you want anything or what?"

He's asking if I . . . *want* anything? I want more things than I can name. I want this drive never to have happened, this bridge never crossed. I want Cheryl to stay on her side of the river, and my dad on mine. I want my mom and dad back together, but that goes without saying. I even want Casey home from soccer camp, if that'll help return things to normal. I want a life nothing like a noir movie. I want to find out Jackson had no strange girl in the projection booth with him. That he's in Shanosha right now eating ice cream with his girlfriend, Elissa, and that doesn't bother me in the slightest because if he's going to be with anyone, it should be Elissa. I want to be assured that everything's as it should be, that everything's fine. I want no lies and all truth, all the time. That's what I want.

So I let my eyes come open. First one, then the other. The sight is blinding. What an ugly house Cheryl has, with sickly green floodlights, and concrete instead of grass on the lawn, and flat, smeary windows decorated with . . . boxes of cereal?

Oh, this isn't the house. It's a convenience store.

"We need eggs," Dad says. He has his car door open, waiting for my answer. "Do you want anything from in there or not?"

Rita Hayworth would not want a thing. She'd stay strong and wouldn't be lured by the bright lights and shelves of convenience. But Rita Hayworth was a movie star—she never got thirsty like regular people. She wouldn't cave.

I, on the other hand . . .

"Chocolate milk," I burst out. "I really want some chocolate milk." These are the first words I've spoken in close to an hour.

"Then come on in," Dad says.

And I unbuckle my seat belt, and, with the last ounce of pride I have left, I open my car door and lead the way in.

Cheryl's actual house—the house Dad now lives in—is not as ugly as a convenience store, but I take the time to notice as many questionable things as I can. It's only fair to my mom, even if she did have a hand in sending me here for the weekend.

Ugly things spotted: ugly gold vase holding ugly bigheaded flowers, ugly brown carpet leading up the stairs, ugly picture of a horse in the hallway, ugly refrigerator magnets, ugly curtains, ugly deformed-looking knobs on all the doors.

I'd like to say Cheryl is as ugly as her house, but that would be a lie. She's okay, I guess. She is blond and pointy, with long arms and long fingers, and she obviously straightens her hair because I notice a frizzy curl she missed at the back.

She has a blond and pointy sixteen-year-old daughter named Nichole. I haven't met her yet, but I know what she looks like from the pictures in the stairwell. Her name's not Nicole but Nic-*hole*—I see the nameplate on her bedroom door.

"Is she in there?" I say as we stand outside her closed door.

Cheryl looks anxiously at the door, but she doesn't knock on it. "You'll meet her later," she says, avoiding the question. Then she sweeps me down the hall toward another door, which she opens with a flourish. "This," Cheryl says, "is *your* room."

She points to it, her smile eating up a full half of her face, as if she expects me to leap inside and lick the walls.

"I already have a room," I say. I don't budge from my spot in the hallway. Cheryl's just my dad's girlfriend—I don't understand why she's acting like this has to be my house too.

"I know you have a room at home," Cheryl says. "But this is your room here."

She switches on the light to reveal four walls, one tiny window, and a prison mattress. (Fine, a canopy bed, but I decide that if and when I recount this later I will tell everyone about the prison mattress.) The room is so small it fits just the bed and a dresser. You'd have to walk sideways to reach the window. You'd have to hold your breath if you wanted to do anything more.

"I don't need two rooms," I say.

"You can decorate it any way you like," she says, her voice getting higher and louder with each word. "Right, honey?"

I flinch.

My dad, aka "honey," has been hovering during this conversation. He holds my little suitcase. "It's your room," he says. "I want you to feel at home here."

If I puked, it would fade in to match the blech color of the hall carpet, I realize. If I puked here and now at what my dad just said, you could walk this hall for years and never know it.

I take one step into the room. "It's huge!" I say.

"Danielle," my dad admonishes me. I guess he still knows me well enough to detect my sarcasm.

I sit on the bed and give it a good bounce. "Wow," I say. "What was this room before, a shoe closet?"

Cheryl looks aghast. That's when I realize it probably was her closet. I bet she had to move all her stuff to the basement so I could have a room to sleep in. Her winter clothes and shoes are gathering mold in the basement, all for me!

"Thanks for letting me use your closet, Cheryl," I say with the utmost politeness. "I *really* appreciate it."

"Danielle, please," my dad says. He makes me feel bad. Almost.

"You have your own bathroom," Cheryl says out of the blue. She's quite possibly deranged. She opens a door to reveal the bathroom and then smiles, all her teeth showing.

"Actually . . ." she adds. "You share the bathroom with Nichole." She motions toward a closed door at the opposite end of the bathroom, just beside the toilet. "It connects to her room too." Then she turns to my dad. "I'll leave you two to get settled in."

When she steps out, it's just me and Dad, Dad and me, chillin' in a closet. I'd say it's just like old times, but it's not. Not at all.

"Is this how it's going to be all weekend?" Dad says.

"Like what?" I say innocently.

"When your brother comes to visit I hope he's on better behavior."

"Casey will love it here. Does he get his own closet too?"

Dad lets out a long, low sigh. I'm his test case, I see now. I'm the first piece from his old life that's come spilling into his new. Maybe he should have thought some on this before carting me over. Or at least waited before buying the canopy bed.

"Go ahead and unpack," he says at last. "Come down when you're ready." Then he leaves, just like that. He doesn't yell at me for being so awful. He doesn't tell me to appreciate my closet because some kids in the world have no food and nowhere to live and they don't even *have* closets. He's just gone, like he's flat-out given up on me.

This is all his fault. Could someone tell me why *I* feel bad?

I'm alone not two seconds when the door beside the toilet flips open and a girl shoves through the bathroom to gawk at me. Nichole is a younger version of her mom, her hair long, her jeans low on her hips the way my mom would never let me wear them. Her eyes are like the sharp little stones you step on when you're running down the driveway to get the mail and you thought you didn't need your shoes but you so totally regret it.

She speaks first. "That's my bed." She shoots her gaze at the canopy. "I didn't want it anymore so they stuck it in here."

"Okay," I say. What, am I supposed to be grateful?

She continues. "So you're not going to be my sister. Got it?"

"Got it," I say, like it's her choice what we are and we aren't. Like I would ever think that sleeping on her hand-me-down bed makes us sisters somehow. For some reason, my mouth won't open to say that.

There's something about Nichole that makes me nervous. Maybe because she's older and has on those great jeans. Or maybe it's because this is her house and not mine.

So I add, "I never thought we would be sisters."

She takes me in for a beat. "Huh," she says. "You haven't seen the ring."

"What ring?"

"What?" she says.

"What?" I say.

"Whatever," she says. She's toying with me. "So how old are you again, twelve?"

"Thirteen," I say, mortally offended. "I'm going into eighth grade."

She doesn't seem too impressed. "Where?"

"Shanosha." The name of my public school is the same as the name of my town, fashioned after some Native American word I'm not even sure is for real. It's a school in the middle of nowhere full of middle-of-nowhere kids. I wonder if she knows that.

She sniffs. I guess she does.

She doesn't tell me what grade she's in or where she goes to school. She just says, "If this door is closed"—she indicates the door from my room into the bathroom—"you don't open it. I'll let you know when and if you're allowed in. You use that sink and don't touch my sink. You'd better have brought your own toothpaste, I swear. If you *have* to take a shower do it before nine, so you're not in my way. And no baths. Not ever. The only person who takes a bath in that tub is me."

She's acting like I'm going to spend all my time here, in this bathroom.

"Okay?" she says.

"Yeah, okay, no problem."

I can't figure out how I can snap out whatever thing I want when it's to my mom or my dad or even my dad's girlfriend, Cheryl, but just being around Nichole turns me meek. *No problem?* I don't even know who I am anymore.

She heads back into the bathroom.

"Hey, Nichole?" I say, my voice all squeaky.

"Yeah?"

"What ring?"

She takes one last look at me and slams the door in my face.

Fine. If this were a movie, I guess I wouldn't even be in it.

I sit beneath the pink prison canopy, alone. I have a bad feeling. I can barely breathe. I grab my bag and dig through it for my phone. This house may be on the other side of the river, which is so far from home it feels like the other side of the world, but at least it's down out of the mountains, in civilization. I bet it gets perfect cell-phone reception.

Only—I can't find my phone.

I dump the contents of my bag out on the bed. Lots of old

ticket stubs plus a few bits of stale popcorn. The broken headphones that go with my iPod but not the iPod itself. Wintergreen gum. Spearmint gum. A blue pencil swiped from my mom's office, eraserless. My house key. A plastic spoon from Taco Juan's, licked clean.

But nothing even remotely pink. Which means no phone.

Then I picture it, exactly where I left it. Theater 1, right side, second row, up close and personal to the screen. My cell phone is sitting on the arm of that seat just where I left it. It couldn't be anywhere else.

I retrace my steps to be sure. *Touch of Evil* started playing, I looked back at the projection booth, I saw—I don't know what I saw—and I must have lost my head and run out of the theater before grabbing the phone.

I've got to call the Little Art to see if my cell is still there. If I do, there are three things that could happen. One, Ms. Greenway picks up. She says she has my phone and to cheer me up she promises to hold all Rita Hayworth movies until I'm back home.

Two, Austin picks up. He's his usual obnoxious self and we fight for hours and I run screaming from the conversation before even finding out if he has my phone.

Then there's three: Jackson picks up. I could ask about my phone, but shouldn't I ask about something—some*one*—else? I don't know if I'd have the guts to do it.

I'm searching out a landline when I'm caught red-handed in my dad's bedroom. I've just touched my fingers to the phone on the bedside table when my dad's voice comes at me from the doorway. "What are you doing in here?" he says.

"Just using the phone," I say. But he pulls me out of the room, and I realize he thinks I was in there snooping. He thinks I'm paying attention to the fact that Cheryl's got an ugly orange-yellow blanket on the bed, like I'll go reporting that little detail back to Mom.

I have to ask him. "Nichole said something about a ring—" I start.

"Nichole told you that?" he cuts in.

"Yeah."

"*I* wanted to be the one to tell you that. On the drive here I thought we'd come to a place where we could—"

Now I'm the one to interrupt. "What ring?" I ask. "Like, a ring for Cheryl? An engagement ring?"

Instead of answering, his eyes skitter back into the bedroom. To the dresser. To a box on top of the dresser. A small black velvet box. Inside is probably some sparkly thing, barely even ugly at all, and I don't want to set my eyes on it, not ever.

"Yes," he says at last. "That's what it is."

"Why isn't she wearing it?" I ask. "Did she say she has to think about it?"

I hope that's what she said. Here's to hoping she wanted to meet me first before deciding to marry my dad. And now that she has, and sees how difficult I am, she'll say it's off and we'll go back to our side of the river and never come here again.

"In fact," he says, "she said yes." His face is all red. Flushed with shame, maybe, flushed with happiness. Probably both. "She just thought I should talk to you first before she wore the ring in front of you."

I turn away. I will never look at Cheryl's fingers again.

"What do you think about this, Dani? Tell me what you're thinking."

Dad so does not want to know what I'm thinking.

Out of all the vicious things that could come spilling out of my mouth at this moment in time—a moment I'm sure I'll remember always, my heart sunk as low as my feet into the hideous depths of the hall carpet—what I say is, "I just need to use a phone."

"What happened to the cell phone I bought you? Did you lose it?"

"I forgot to charge the battery," I say quickly. "And I didn't pack the adapter."

He accepts this as fact and leads me down to the cordless phone in the kitchen. I grab it and retreat back upstairs to the room they call my room. Once I'm in there, door closed, phone in hand, losing oxygen in that tight, sealed space, I realize how easy it had been.

To lie.

I keep doing it. These lies—kittens and cell phones—they just slip out. I could have told the truth, but I didn't. I let that little white lie escape my lips and, without a beat, Dad believed me. Lying is far easier than I realized. Maybe once you become a teenager you get a knack for lying. You become more skilled in lies the older you get, so by the time you're grown up with kids and a house and a marriage, it's all you know how to do about anything: lie and lie and lie some more. I guess I'll be an expert by then.

I push all thoughts of the engagement away and call the Little Art. Austin picks up. I'm relieved that it's not Jackson until he starts talking.

"I heard you're in big trouble," Austin says. "Are you grounded?"

"I'm at my dad's house. That's worse than being grounded."

"Oh," he says, and pauses like he wants to say something else. Austin has a dad too. He must have one—how else could he exist to annoy me? But I realize I've never asked him where his dad is. I could. I could go ahead and ask. Maybe Austin wants me to. Maybe his dad did what mine's doing now. Out of all the people I know, Austin might be the one to understand. . . .

"My dad—" I say. I fumble over how to put it. "My dad, he—"

I can't, though. There really is no way to put it.

"What?" Austin says.

"My dad made me call. You know that cell phone he got me? I left it in the theater. Could you go get it?"

"Are you sure you left it here? Did you check your bag?"

"It's there. Second row, on the right side. Just go get it."

"Are you *sure*? I don't want to go all the way down there if you're not sure."

I let out a sigh, can't help it. Austin. He drives me *insane*. Why would I ever think of confiding anything in him?

"Yes. I am *sure*. Go get it, Austin. I'll wait."

"You're always telling me what to do," he says. I expect more of an argument, but there's only the clatter of the phone as he drops it and stomps away.

I wait. I wait and wait and wait. Austin sure is taking his time. He probably found the phone right away but decided to stretch out on a seat, kick back, watch a bit of the movie. Then he probably decided to get himself some popcorn. Then do some jumping jacks. I don't know—what's taking him so long?

The line crackles as he picks up at last. "Hey, who's this?" he mumbles.

"It's me, Dani. So did you find it or what?"

But I spoke too soon. Though the idea of Austin conking his head in the dark theater and stumbling away with amnesia so he forgot who he was talking to is funny, it's not what's happening. This isn't Austin.

"Oh, hey, D," the voice on the other end of the line says. "What's up?"

It's Jackson, the big liar himself.

6

What's in Black-and-White

"*So you think you lost your phone, huh?*" Jackson says.

"I don't *think* I lost it, I know I lost it," I say. Here's my chance. "Jackson . . . You know in the theater before? I thought I saw—"

"The car blew up," he says. "Was that sweet or what?"

I step up to the window, part the ugly curtains, look out at the backyard. All I see are trees—just like at my house. It's freaky how the trees here are exactly like my trees, how for one second I can look out this window and think I'm home.

"Not the movie," I tell Jackson—though I'm glad he cleared up the mystery of what that fuzzy thing on screen was supposed to be. "I mean in real life."

"What're you talking about?" There's a faint shift in his voice. I hear it, just like a noir detective might hear it. This is how I know Jackson knows I know, you know?

"I thought I saw someone," I say carefully. "In the projection booth with you."

"Nah," Jackson says. "That was me."

So we're going to play it that way, are we?

In my memory the picture is clear: two silhouettes, two heads, which adds up to—you guessed it—two separate people. Unless Jackson grew a second head, someone was there was him.

"I thought I saw a girl," I say.

"What girl?"

"I *saw* her. She had on pink tights, with polka dots." And though it's true I saw a girl—on the street, not in the projection booth—he doesn't need to know that little detail. "Not Elissa," I say, so he doesn't try that on me. "A girl who wasn't Elissa."

"Oh, yeah! I forgot. I ordered pizza and some girl came by to deliver it."

"What kind of pizza?" I ask suspiciously.

"Pepperoni and peppers, what else?" he says, as if I should know.

And just like that, I begin to doubt myself. Maybe I want to doubt myself because it's Jackson, of all people. So I come up with different scenarios where Austin was distracted—he did admit he went to the bathroom—and the girl with the pizza slipped through. And then, of course, I ask myself, Shouldn't a pizza-delivery girl wear some kind of uniform, and not funny tights? And isn't it odd that the pizza-delivery girl left out the fire door and not the front? And that she took off in the exact opposite direction of Pie-in-the-Sky, the only pizza joint in town? So now I'm doubting my doubts about myself, and I'm back to doubting Jackson.

"By the way," Jackson says, "don't worry about your cell phone. I was kidding before. I found it on the seat. We'll hang on to it for you."

"Thanks," I say, "but Jackson—"

Before I can finish he mumbles, "Austin wants to talk to you." Even though I shout, "Jackson!" he's no longer listening. He's handed the phone over to his cousin.

"Why'd you have me look all over the theater if Jackson had your phone the whole time?" Austin asks, sounding seriously fed up.

I'm about to respond, but I'm distracted by the sense that I'm not alone. I turn to find the bathroom door wide open. Nichole's in the doorway, wielding a flatiron in one hand. She does her hair and stares at me. I wonder how long she's been here.

"I have to go," I tell Austin.

"Fine," he says, "but you really need to be more careful with your—" I hang up.

"I heard you yelling," Nichole says. "Jackson who? Jackson who moved to Shanosha for the summer?" She's *really* staring at me now, like she can see straight through my clothes.

"Jackson Greenway. He's my . . . friend. Do you know him?"

"Really" is all she says, the smallest of smiles on her lips. She presses the flatiron down a length of hair and there's a hot hiss, a sizzle.

"So my dad told me," I say, "about th—" I start, but she's already stepped back inside the bathroom and slammed the door.

"—ring," I finish.

To survive the weekend, I will need TV. But there's no TV in my closet, so I'm watching the classic movie station in the den. In *Laura* everyone loves Laura, and I mean everyone. She has two guys who love her, not to mention her own maid, who loves every crumb she picks up. Even the cop investigating Laura's murder loves her, and that's before he discovers she might not be dead. I can't imagine being someone who's loved that much.

In *Laura*, there's a painted portrait of Laura on the wall that everyone stares at after she's gone. I just want to say that I've noticed—from a quick sweep of Cheryl's house—that nowhere on the walls is there a photo of me.

I'm in the middle of *Laura* when my dad takes a seat on the couch beside me.

"You're not watching this, are you?" he says. He grabs the remote and starts flipping through channels.

I sigh. "I *was*."

"I didn't know you liked those old movies." Didn't know, or didn't care? "I was thinking we could go out," he says. To talk, I'm thinking, he wants to talk. But he says, "Do something fun." He shuts off the TV.

I'm used to this kind of treatment. Grown-ups think that what they want is way more important than what you want. I'm almost fourteen, but to him I'm a kid. And when you're considered a kid, this is how it is. You could be totally engrossed in a movie—like, is that Laura who just came in; wait, is she still alive?—but who cares, the news is on. Let's just say if a grown-up wants to watch the news, you'll watch the news. If a grown-up wants chicken for dinner, grab your fork because you'll be eating chicken. You can't make your own choices, watch your own TV channels, or eat your own food until the world freezes over or, I don't know, college.

So my dad wanted to bond this weekend. Which is how we end up, just the two of us, on the muddy shore of the Hudson throwing sticks for Cheryl's dog.

The dog is a golden retriever but not a very nice one. It doesn't like me. Every time I send a stick sailing, it gives me a look like, *Please tell me you're joking.*

From this side of the river, I can see the other shore, my shore. The divide feels greater than ever.

Dad comes up behind me. It's like he expects something, some make-up moment I'm to remember for the rest of my life. Either that or he wants me to throw him a stick.

"This wasn't what I thought it would be," he says.

"The river does smell something awful," I agree.

"Not the river. This. The weekend."

Oh, I get it. He's playing the kid and I'm playing the adult.

Now I'm supposed to say something to make *him* feel better. I don't, though. I don't say a thing.

"The wedding's in October," he says.

The wedding. There's this quick flash of a poufy white dress and a flying bouquet, a sharp knife slicing a big fat cake. Scenes from a horror movie. I shut my eyes tight.

"I know this is the first time you've met Cheryl, but you'll like her, you'll see. I wanted you two to get to know each other before she became your stepmother."

Did you hear that? He said "stepmother."

Besides, it's not really the first time I met Cheryl—he just may not remember it. I saw her once, before Dad left Mom. I saw her, and it meant nothing then, but it means everything now. That's why I can't let go of the girl in the polka-dot tights. Because I know what happens when you do nothing. Someone gets hurt.

"Does Mom know?" I ask him. "About October?"

"Yes," he says softly. "She knows."

I see Cheryl's dog coming back up the riverbank. I take a short stick and with all my might shoot it out as far as I can manage, maybe into the water, maybe all the way across to the other side. The dog looks at me with contempt and then runs off after it.

Dad says, "Tell me what you want from me, Danielle."

You know this scene in the movie. Things will be said, but, don't worry, all will be tied up in a bow in five minutes, tops. Tears will evaporate like they'd never been shed, the dad will say *Forgive me* and the daughter will say *I do,* the sun will shine, the dog will retrieve the stick, the music will play, the credits will roll. The end.

But I'm shutting down the projector and starting my own movie. Here goes.

"I'm not going," I say.

"You're not what?"

"I'm not going. In October. You can't make me."

"Of course you're going," he insists.

"I'm not!" I shriek. Then I get serious and say, quieter, "I'm not."

I've said it, and he looks shocked, so I decide to say some more. I see big trouble in my future, grounding by water torture, grounding by fire, but I have to add one last bit, the cherry on top of my angry sundae, and say I hate him for what he did and I'll never forgive him, never.

He has a dazed, empty look in his eyes. I've stunned him to silence. There's nothing more to be said after what I confessed—or wait, no. Now he's talking.

"Have you seen the dog?" he says.

"She went off that way." I point to where I pitched the stick.

"She should be back by now," he says. And he calls her name, "Gloria! Gloria!"—a ridiculous name for a dog—and goes down the riverbank to search for her.

Gloria's not barking. I can't see her anywhere. The stick I threw may have landed in the river. I may have just drowned my soon-to-be stepmother's dog.

I start down the riverbank looking for her. I'm walking past the parking lot when I spot Gloria. There she is, beside my dad's car, stick in mouth, waiting for us. I don't know what happened to my dad, so I just go to Gloria and plop down on the curb beside her.

"What should I do?" I say, not caring that I'm talking to a dog.

Gloria opens her mouth to drop the stick. She doesn't want me to throw it again—she wants to show me her jaws.

"I don't really hate him," I tell her. "I'm just feeling all weird. And sometimes you say things you don't mean when you're feeling weird."

Gloria snorts. She stares me down with her cold canine eyes.

"I don't have to go in October, do I?"

She snorts again, softer this time.

"He never should have lied," I say. "This is what you get when you lie."

Gloria slumps down to sniff the concrete. She may not care what I have to say—she may be a dog and technically not even able to understand what I have to say—but I need at least one living thing to tell it to.

My dad comes up then and I could repeat it all back to him, but I don't. In the movies, people talk to each other because otherwise you'd have nothing to watch. But here, on this side of the river, we don't talk about anything.

The big nothing between us is carried to the car. It travels with us down the road and back to the house, and once there it squeezes itself onto the love seat in the den while I watch TV.

Some movies I could be watching on the classic movie station this Sunday afternoon: *Detour. D.O.A. The Stranger. The Maltese Falcon. The Man Who Cheated Himself. The Woman in the Window. The Man Who Made Up a Big Fat Lie.* (I invented that last one.)

It could be any of those, I'm not sure what. Nichole just walked in front of the TV.

"You can't seriously be watching this," she says. "Where's the remote?"

Now, normally, I would never give up the remote control. When my brother and I had a war over the remote, I once chucked it down the garbage disposal before letting him have it. (Mom rescued it before it got ground to bits.) I also shoved it so far down into the cushions of the pull-out couch that it wasn't found until weeks later when my uncle Lou came to stay for Thanksgiving.

But Nichole sets me on edge. Tonight she has her long hair down, knife-straight. And worse, she's brought a friend. The friend has honey-colored hair, a faint smirk, and stands there feverishly sending text messages instead of acknowledging that I'm here in the room.

The remote is in my lap. Nichole sees it there and opens her hand, palm up and fingers fluttering, like, *Give it here.* And I do give it, like I've got no spine. I've barely let go and the picture on the TV goes from beautiful black-and-white to hyper color, like a demented carnival has overrun the room. In other words, Nichole switched the channel to a romantic comedy.

I get up off the couch. My mom will be here soon anyway.

"Where're you going, Dani?" Nichole says. "I want you to meet my friend."

I stop in the middle of the room. Some actress incomparable to Rita Hayworth pretends to cry on-screen. She needs some help—I don't see a single tear. Word of advice: Try sticking your face in an onion.

"This is Kelsey," Nichole says.

Kelsey sniffs and looks up from her phone for the first time. I like her shirt—it's white and has these great huge sleeves you could hide a ham in—but I don't have to tell her that so I just sniff back. Kelsey's sniff was half disinterest, half disdain. Mine sounded like I caught a cold.

"Kelsey, this is Dani," Nichole continues. "You know who she's friends with? *Jackson*."

"No way," says Kelsey.

"Way," says Nichole.

This is totally rehearsed. Why should Nichole care who I'm friends with?

"So do you know Jackson or what?" I say.

"We know him," Nichole says.

"We know his girlfriend," adds Kelsey.

"So do I," I say.

"How do you know Bella?" Kelsey asks.

"Who?" I say. "Jackson's girlfriend is *Elissa*."

"She doesn't even know his girlfriend's name," Nichole tells Kelsey. "She's making it all up."

"She's weird," says Kelsey. "Who is she again, your stepsister?"

"Ugh, not *yet*," Nichole says. Then she turns back to me. "If you really do know Jackson, where's he been? He never comes around anymore."

"He's working," I say. Even as I make an excuse for Jackson, I wonder if I should. Am I giving him an alibi? If so, for what?

"Working all the time, yeah, right," Kelsey says. "That's what he tells Bella."

"He's saving for a car," I put in. "You know, one of those really old ones with the wings." This shuts Kelsey up—if she knows Jackson, she knows that's true. "I mean fins," I add. Then, "Who's Bella?"

"C'mon, Kelsey," Nichole says, and they flounce out. It takes me a few moments to figure out that they took the remote with them.

I'm a little afraid all of a sudden. Not just because I'm stuck in a room with a cheesy romantic comedy and I don't have the remote to shut it off. And not just because that rude girl with the bad taste in movies is about to become my stepsister. But also because of what they just said. I'm afraid I might know who Bella is. Might she, sometimes, walk around in the middle of the summer wearing a pair of polka-dot tights?

I can't think straight. The romantic comedy is so loud it's rotting my brain. I go up to the TV to change the channel manually. I get so close to the screen I see spots.

My mom rescues me within the hour. As soon as I see her hatchback pull into the driveway I leap off the front porch and go sailing straight for it.

My dad stands in the driveway to see us off. The distance between him and my mom is the length of a mountain bike. They won't get any closer than that.

I wait for my dad to tell my mom all the awful things I said to him—it'll give them something to talk about, selecting my punishment. But he doesn't, maybe because he knows my mom might agree. He just says bye and waves us out of the driveway like it never happened.

"How'd it go?" Mom asks once we reach the highway. She's trying so hard not to show any emotion, she's barely moving her mouth when she speaks.

I want to tell her that I know—about the ring, about October. But instead, I say, "They locked me in a closet, I drowned Cheryl's dog, and I told Dad I hate him." That'll keep her updated.

She laughs for the first time—she thinks I'm joking.

And then, to cheer her up even more, I list all the ugly things I spotted in Cheryl's house. I've had the whole weekend to catalog, so the list is long. I'm still in the middle of it when we reach the Rhinecliff Bridge: ugly vase, ugly table napkins, ugly mailbox, ugly light switches, ugly garden hose, ugly . . .

I could keep going, but it occurs to me that my mom is either enthralled by her rival's ugliness or else she's not listening. I peek over at Mom as we reach the middle of the bridge. She looks pained.

I could recite a few hundred more ugly things, but I keep them to myself and roll down the window instead. The scent of mud carries in off the Hudson and I breathe it in, deeply. The bridge ends, and we're back on our side of the river. We're home.

7

The Pie in the Sky

H*ere I am,* unpacking in my actual bedroom in the actual house where I actually live, when the scariest thing happens.

It's so scary I drop my suitcase, so scary I almost scream. I feel like I'm in one of those dreams where you're stuck in slow motion and you see this horrible creature coming at you (a giant spider with scissors for fangs, but everything's blurry so it might just be a big dog). And you know you're sleeping, but you can't make yourself wake up. And your shoes are untied (that happens a lot in my dreams) and you can't get your feet to move and— You get the picture.

What could possibly be that scary, you ask?

I look up and Austin Greenway is standing in my room.

"How did you get in here?" I shriek. Technically he's not inside the room—he's standing just outside of it in the hallway. But still.

"Your mom said I could come up," he says, voice all shaky. "I brought your phone." Now he's acting like I'm the one who scared *him*.

"Don't you ever do anything like that again."

"What? Bring you *your* phone that *you* left at *my* house?"

"I left it in the theater, not at your house."

"Same difference. It's the same building."

I roll my eyes. I try to think back to what I was doing before I saw him. I'd dumped out my suitcase. I was biting off a fingernail. I was probably thinking about something serious, like stepmothers or pizza. So was he just standing here the whole time, watching me *think*?

"Do you want the phone back or not?" he says. He's still in the hallway as if he assumes I'm going to hit him if he steps inside the room. And you know what? I might.

"Just leave the phone and go," I say.

I expect a lecture. Something like how I can't assume he'll be my own personal messenger service. That next time I leave something I'll have to go get it myself.

But he doesn't say any of that. He just crouches down and places my pink cell phone on the floor about an inch inside my doorway. Then he turns to go back downstairs.

I wonder if I made him feel the way Nichole made me feel. I'm no Nichole. Anyway, I don't want to be.

"Austin," I say. With great effort, I spit out, "That was really nice of you to come all the way out here to bring me my phone. Thank you."

He turns back. He picks up the phone and carries it into the room. Not only that, he takes this as permission to start talking.

"It's really only five point four minutes on a bike," he says. "I clocked it. I took a shortcut through Upper Canyon and down Ridge. Ever try that way?"

"Of course," I say automatically. "I live here."

Uh-oh. Shouldn't have answered. Now he thinks I've invited him to stay. He's taken a seat on my chair. Next thing you know he'll want me to fetch him an iced tea.

"So when does Casey get back?" he asks. Casey's been gone for a month and won't be back for weeks and thank you very much, Austin, for bringing him up.

"The week before school starts," I say.

"Does he call a lot?" he asks. I realize he's still holding my phone. He came by to return it, but he can't keep his grimy mitts off of it. "Because he didn't call all weekend. Neither did Maya. . . . I kept it charged—my phone uses the same kind of charger—and I checked, in case you called me to ask."

"Let me see," I say. I grab the phone and wave it out the window so it picks up two bars of reception. He's right: no missed calls, no voice mails, not even a text.

"I guess Casey's real busy, huh?" Austin says. "He's so lucky. I wish I could've gone to soccer camp."

"You do? In gym class you got hit in the face with the ball that time you were supposed to be goalie."

"You saw that?" he mumbles.

I shrug.

"What I mean is I wish I could *play* soccer so I could go to soccer camp. Staying in town all summer . . . it stinks."

This is the first time it occurs to me that Austin might be

bored too. I guess I figured he was having a blast this summer, counting tickets and playing walkie-talkie.

So I give him one thing. One tiny thing I hope he doesn't hold over me later. Once said out loud, he'll know how much it means to me. But I say it anyway. "At least we'll always have the Little Art."

"Yeah," he says, looking at me, "at least."

He tries to meet my eyes, but I won't let it happen.

"I'm not just here to return the phone, you know," he says. "I actually came by to tell you something else. There've been these weird calls to the Little Art. . . . Some girl. She calls asking for Jackson, but she never gives her name."

"Oh?" I say lightly.

"Um, yeah. So, like I said, she won't give her name. If Jackson's not around, if he's busy working or something, she'll just go 'sorry, wrong number,' and hang up."

"And you're sure it's not Elissa?"

"I know Elissa's voice!" Austin says, then softens. "I thought it was Elissa at first too, but then the girl called when I was talking to Elissa and that would have been scientifically impossible so I've ruled out Elissa. It has to be someone else."

I know something. The name of the girl. But I'm not yet

ready to reveal that to Austin. I'd like to get all the information I can out of him first.

"How long has she been calling?" I ask.

"Weeks."

"Weeks! This has been going on for weeks and you didn't tell me?"

"I don't have to tell you everything," he says, all defensive. He picks up a book from off my floor and flips through it. It's not like he wants to read it—he's just doing it to bother me. "I thought you'd be interested because of that girl you said you saw. In the projection booth. Do you think it was her, the one who's calling?"

Yes, of course that's what I think. But I tell him what Jackson told me. "I asked him about that. He said it was just some delivery girl. He ordered pizza." I shrug. "I guess that could be true," I add. "I guess he could have ordered a pizza. . . ."

I don't say that I *want* it to be true. I want there to be some reasonable explanation for the visit, for the phone calls, for everything. Once one person you trust up and lies, you don't want to have to go through it again with someone else. Once you see one person hurt, you wouldn't wish it on anyone—especially not someone as sweet as Elissa.

But Austin's not buying it. "Pizza? That's impossible," he says.

"You can't say that. It's *possible.* Who's to say he didn't want a pizza? You said yourself you left the lobby to go to the bathroom. So the pizza-delivery girl could have slipped by when you weren't looking. . . ."

Austin shakes his head. "I'm telling you, Dani, there is no way Jackson ordered a pizza."

"How can you be so sure?"

"Because," he says. "Because Jackson doesn't eat pizza."

"Who doesn't eat pizza?" I burst out.

"People who are seriously lactose intolerant," he shoots back. "It runs in the family." Then he coughs, as if for effect.

I don't know what to say to that.

"Anyway," Austin says, "so the girl called this weekend. I told Jackson to come get the phone. He was really annoyed and said why can't people call his cell phone. So I said, I don't know maybe because your cell phone doesn't work in the theater and that's why you have to use the walkie-talkies like I've been telling you and . . ."

He sees the look on my face and gets on with it.

"So I gave him the phone and left him alone. Then I

heard him yelling. When I came back he'd punched a hole in the wall."

"No," I say. "He wouldn't do that. I don't believe it."

Austin says, like it doesn't matter if I believe it or not, "Then go see for yourself." He starts picking through the stuff I dropped on my floor: a tube of lip gloss, a comb, my broken iPod headphones.

I don't say anything at first. I'm thinking. I'm thinking how, if this were a movie, Jackson would be in deep trouble right about now.

In the movie, the detective and her irritating sidekick would be talking in their dark office. "We've got him," they'd say, gathering up enough evidence to break the case wide open.

And across town the suspect would be crossing a street, but he'd get all paranoid. He'd run and hide in an alley. He'd be concealing his left hand in his pocket. The knuckles would be bandaged up, like he just punched a hole through a wall.

Only, in the movie the suspect wouldn't be, couldn't be, someone like Jackson. He wouldn't be the guy with cool taste in movies. The guy who rides the red bike around town. The guy who listens when you talk. Who looks at you like you matter. The guy who's dating your babysitter, so you probably shouldn't be thinking such things. No movie would do a thing like that.

"What are you thinking?" Austin says.

"I'm thinking when are you going to stop touching my stuff and leave my room?"

"Okay," Austin says, dropping one of my pens. "I thought you'd like to know, that's all. If you want me to leave, I'll leave." He says this and stands up, waiting for me to give the definitive answer.

"Austin," I say. "Leave."

I have my back turned when he finally goes. I wait a good minute before heading downstairs to make sure he's gone. There's no sign of him out the windows. I don't see his bike on the road.

"Was Austin going to stay for dinner?" my mom asks. She appears behind me, standing by the banister, looking distracted.

"Of course not," I say, horrified. Then I see my mom's face. I see it, like, really see it, for the first time since she picked me up at Dad's. She's not okay.

Gently, I lead her away from the stairs and into the living room. We sit on the couch. It's getting dark, and I have to turn the lamp on. We have the whole house to ourselves for another night. Outside, the chirps of crickets have begun, and a car drives by every once in a while, but beneath that? It's called quiet. It's what happens when you live in Shanosha where no one wants to be. All of a sudden it feels so lonely. Almost like it would have been nice to have someone over for dinner.

"What's for dinner?" I ask my mom.

At first I don't know if she heard me. She's staring into space. Then I realize she's not staring at nothing. She's looking at a water bottle that somehow found its way onto the mantel over the fireplace. The bottle's hidden behind a vase. Someone must have set the bottle there temporarily and forgotten about it.

"That's your father's," she says.

"It's a bottle of water," I say. It could be anybody's.

"It's his," she insists. "From when he lived here. From when he used to go mountain-biking." She takes a breath. "On Saturdays."

Now we're both staring at it. It's half-full. I realize that the spit mixed up inside the bottle could very well be my dad's. He did bring water bottles with him when he went riding on weekends. The bike hasn't been in the garage for months, but the bottle could have been here the whole time. Who knows how long we'd been in and out of this room, sitting on this couch, watching that TV, with that soggy old water up there collecting algae.

Maybe. Or someone else—who knows, even me—left the bottle up there last week and my mom's making a huge big deal out of nothing.

"I'm going to put it in the recycling," I tell her, getting to my feet.

"No," she says. "I'll clean it up." But she makes no move to clean it up. She just sits there, staring at it, like she's practicing her telekinesis and wants to make it do a few loop-the-loops through the room first.

I don't have the heart to argue, so I sit back down.

"He told you, I take it," she says. "He told you he's marrying Cheryl."

"Uh-huh," I say. And I wait. I wait for her to say how awful that is. How if I don't want to go to the wedding I totally don't have to go to the wedding.

Only, she doesn't say anything like that. She says nothing. Nothing at all.

It's Sunday night. I'm afraid my mom could stay here on the couch till morning, staring at the mantel. Maybe the weekend was just as hard on her as it was on me.

Still, she'll have to pull herself together. She has work tomorrow. Also, I'm hungry and it's time for dinner.

"Mom," I say. "Dinner, remember? What're we having?"

"I don't know, Dani. I'm sorry, I forgot about it. Did you say Austin's staying?"

"He went home," I say softly.

"That's right," she says.

I'm not sure what to do. Should I throw the water bottle out the window? Dump it over her head and hope it shocks her off the couch and into the kitchen? Is that cruel?

No, wait . . . what I should do is be the one to make dinner. Running through my mind are the things I can cook by myself: scrambled eggs on toast, instant oatmeal, macaroni and cheese from a box. Not too much else.

"Mom?" I say.

"Yeah?"

"Wait here." In the kitchen I discover there's no mac 'n' cheese and only one egg, and the idea of feeding my mom strawberries-and-cream instant oatmeal by the spoonful seems too pitiful to face.

I return to the living room and tell her, "I think we should get pizza."

"Good idea," she says. "There's money in my purse."

The only restaurant in all of Shanosha that delivers is Pie-in-the-Sky, the one pizza joint in town. You could say I'm being a good daughter, making sure my mom gets off the couch and has something to eat. Sure, go ahead, say that. But you and I both know it's really selfish. I'm calling Pie-in-the-Sky for two reasons:

(1) Hello, I am *starving*.

And (2) I want to know if they have a delivery girl working there. A girl who's been known to wear polka-dot tights.

"Pie-in-the-Sky," a high-pitched but utterly bored voice answers. "If you want delivery it'll be at least forty-five minutes. If that's too long, just hang up now."

It's a girl's voice. My heart jumps in my throat. Or else my throat swallows up my heart. Either way, I have a spaz moment and there's some trouble getting my order out.

"Hello?" the bored voice says. Then, "Whatever. I'm hanging up."

I panic so I just blurt out that I want a delivery and I don't care how long it takes and oh, by the way, what are you wearing?

"What did you just say?" says the voice.

"Sorry. Do we know each other, like, have we met before?"

"Duh, I can't see who you are, so how would I know that?"

I tell her who I am, plus my address and phone number,

seeing as she'll need that for the delivery, and then I ask: "Are you the girl who delivers the pizzas?"

The voice on the phone sounds offended. "I am *not* a girl. Why does everyone keep thinking that, jeez!"

Then it dawns on me. "Who is this?"

"It's Tommy, jeez. What kind of pizza do you want or what?"

Tommy. That's the little kid behind the counter. He's maybe eight or nine. Either this town's got a major problem with child-labor laws or his parents own the place and they let him answer the phone. Well, it's not my fault he sounds like a girl.

I give him my order (pepperoni and peppers, I'm curious) and before he can hang up I ask if there's a girl who delivers the pizzas for Pie-in-the-Sky.

And he says, "What girl? Joe will be there in forty-five minutes or less with your pizza," and that's that.

So here I am. No closer to explaining away the girl in the polka-dot tights and just now remembering I don't really even like peppers.

"You didn't just order peppers, did you?" my mom says from the doorway. "I thought you hated peppers."

"'Hate' is a strong word, Mom," I tell her. "I'm trying to give peppers a chance. I'm trying to be mature."

"Really?" my mom says, raising an eyebrow. She's got the start of a smile on her face—which is reason alone to suck down a few peppers, people. "You're trying to be mature now?"

(Is she thinking of the time I "ran away" in protest so I wouldn't have to go to my dad's? Is she thinking of the time she asked me to stay put in the car and I took off after the imaginary kitten?)

"Yes," I say. I grab two plates from the cabinet even though it'll be almost an hour before we can even use them. "So how do you think I'm doing?"

"I think you have a ways to go," she says, then sighs. "But don't we all."

8

Some Things You Might Not Know

H*ere are some things you might not know* about Rita Hayworth. Sure, a lot of people know she started off as a dancer, and that Rita Hayworth wasn't even her real name (it was Margarita Cansino before the movie people made her change it), but there's more.

She was shy. Like, really shy. You wouldn't expect a movie star famous all over the globe to want to stay home instead of go out to parties, but Rita did. She was glamorous on the outside, but inside she was maybe just like you. Or me.

She had trouble with love. She got married and divorced, married and divorced, like five times. One time she married a prince, but even that didn't work out.

When she died, of Alzheimer's, she didn't know who she was. That's the disease where you forget the people you know and the things you once did. That makes me sad, to think Rita didn't know how incredible she was.

Here are some things you might not know about my mom. Right now, all you know is that she cries a lot, and her face looks like a hot-pink balloon when she does, and she's so sensitive, bottles of water can turn her to stone. But she's also funny. She makes me laugh when she's not blowing her nose into a wad of tissues. And she's smart—she wouldn't be managing editor of the town paper if she wasn't.

Her favorite color is blue, that pale turquoise-y blue you can notice in the sky sometimes on a real nice day if you live in the middle of nowhere. I'm not sure what the name of it is. Anyway, a lot of stuff around our house is that color blue. Our mailbox is that color blue. The kitchen cabinets are that color blue. The plates we eat our pizza on are that color blue.

So when my mom is doing okay—picking the peppers off her pepperoni pizza and sticking them on the edge of her blue plate—I tell her that her house is so much prettier than Cheryl's house. I tell her I love her blue curtains and I love her blue candlesticks and I love the blue rug by the door where we wipe off the mud from our shoes. It's the perfect color, I tell her, that muddy rug.

I'm on a roll, but she stops me.

"Dani, you don't have to say all that."

So maybe I'm being too nice. But she needs that right now, don't you think? If you look at her a certain way—like sideways, and while squinting, and if the kitchen lights were a touch dimmer, and if she had her hair up, and lipstick on even though she hardly ever wears lipstick—she might look almost exactly like Rita Hayworth. Almost exactly.

The phone rings and it's my brother, Casey. He tells Mom about soccer camp and I listen to her end of the conversation, picking at my peppers instead of eating them.

"He wants to talk to you," Mom says at last.

I take the cordless and step out of the room for some privacy.

"How's she doing?" he asks. That's the first thing he's said to me in weeks.

"Fine," I say, "I guess."

"Are you taking good care of her? Are you trying not to be a brat?"

"I'm not a brat!"

"Dani. You're forgetting I *know* you."

"Oh and I'm fine too, by the way," I tell him. "I'm doing just great. In case you weren't too busy bouncing balls off your head to wonder about your little sister. I haven't fallen off the face of the earth. I'm not dead."

He's silent for a second. "I heard you went to Dad's," he says. "Dad told me about the wedding."

Now I'm the one who gets silent.

"How bad was it?" he asks. "At his house?"

"Bad," I say.

"Sucks," he says.

"Yup," I say.

And that's all we have to say about that.

We say our good-byes. He tells me to stay out of his room, and I say why would I want to go in there anyway (though I have, to borrow his CDs and to see if he left any money in his dresser), and I shove back into the kitchen and hang up.

"You must miss your brother," Mom says. "And with me, going through"—she waves a hand in the air at absolutely nothing—"all this. And with Maya moving away . . . This must be a really tough summer for you."

Um, hello. Was she walking around all summer with her head in a paper bag?

But I don't say anything mean. Not one thing. I know I'm in a difficult situation and I'm allowed to be difficult, but I kinda don't want to be right now. Casey called me a brat. I'd like to prove that I'm not.

I say, "I guess." Then, "But I'm okay, really."

And she says, "I'll think of something fun for you to do. You can't spend your whole summer sitting in a dark movie theater. It's just not healthy."

That's when I remember Jackson. And the girl, whoever she is. And Elissa. And the phone calls. And the hole punched in the wall. And I get this new determination. This fire inside me. I decide that this will be my mission for the rest of the summer: to find out what's up. And if something awful's going on, to stop it.

There are some things you might not know about me, too. I may daydream more than normal, and make up stuff in my head, and go on and on about movies, but I do know when it's time to stand up and do something real for once.

I take a big bite of my pizza. It's cold by now. And it's covered in green slimy things and all I want to do is spit them out. So now you know I officially really, really don't like peppers. But you should also know that no one's going to lie to me again and get away with it. I won't let it happen. That's a fact.

9

Holes in the Wall

T*he next day,* I head inside the theater without a ticket. I've come before the first show—*The Big Sleep* hasn't started yet, so there's no one (and by that I mean Austin) to tell me to pay or go away.

The house phone is in a hallway off the lobby, a narrow passage just before the stairs up to Ms. Greenway's office. That's where I find Jackson. He's on his knees on the floor, patching up a hole in the wall. He's done enough patching with the spackle that there really isn't a hole anymore. With his back to me, he keeps at it, smoothing the spot. Either his aunt told him to make it neat or he hopes to leave no trace of what he did.

"Hey," I shoot out, startling him.

He jumps, splashing spackle at me. It's stickier than I expected, like egg whites mixed up with gobs of paste.

"Oh, hey, D," he says. "Sorry about that."

I wipe some goop off my arm. "What happened?" I point at the wall.

"Nothing," he says. "I knocked my elbow into it, no big."

Then quickly he adds, "Why, did Austin tell you something else?"

"I don't know, what else would he have told me?"

"I don't know, why don't you say what he told you, and I'll tell you if that's what happened?"

It's one of those nonconversations that get me all tripped up.

His eyes narrow. He is standing up to his full height now, making me feel smaller than I even am. There are a few seconds when I wonder if I should be scared. When I think that maybe something bad's going to happen.

Then it passes. He's grinning. "Dude, I'm such a klutz," he says. He points at my chin. "You've got some glop there. Looks like a white beard."

We laugh. Ha-ha-ha. But I don't know why I'm laughing. I don't know why it's so funny that he punched a hole in the wall and I've got glop on my chin because he threw at it me.

I wipe off my chin. Whatever went on with that wall, it's pretty much all patched up now. You know: like it never even happened.

Jackson puts the lid back on the spackle. "So," he says.

He could admit to anything right now. He could come clean and tell me that he never ordered pizza and he was with some girl named Bella and what would I do then?

But what he says is, "So, how was it at your dad's?"

I give him the same answer I gave my brother: "Bad." I figure he'll say, *That sucks*, and I'll say, *Yeah, that sucks*, and that'll be the end to the conversation. But Jackson sits down on the steps and looks me over.

"What happened?" he asks.

I want to tell him, but first I try not to. "I just didn't want to be there."

"What was it like? Weird, huh?" And somehow, with these questions and more that come after, he gets me talking. It's like he really wants to know how it felt then, what it feels like now. Casey barely asked, and he's my big brother. It's hard to hate Jackson when it seems like he actually cares what I have to say.

He tells me he gets it, that the weekend must have been rough, and I can't explain it. . . . I begin to doubt myself again. Jackson's a good guy. He wouldn't—he couldn't—do what I thought he did. Could he?

"How long have you and Elissa been together?" I find myself asking. I never used to want to talk about Elissa, but everything's changed now.

"It'll be six weeks this weekend," he says with a smile.

"That's forever," I say. In school last year when girls would get boyfriends, it lasted a week, two weeks. That was the longest anyone my age has ever been together.

"You think so?" he says.

"Yeah," I say. "I like Elissa."

"Me too."

"I mean I *really* like Elissa."

"Me too."

I'm trying to say something, but I don't know if he's hearing it. Elissa's the one, I'm saying. I know she's right for him now. I realize he's here for only the summer, but the summer is all that exists right now. And in it, Elissa is the one for him. Which means there can be no one else.

"We should go see her," I say. "Right now."

"Now?" he says. He doesn't move off the steps.

"Let's get ice cream. Let's go say hi to Elissa. You have time, right? The first show isn't until ten forty, right?"

"Right," he says. But he looks torn. "My aunt's out, though. I should stay here."

"But there's no movie playing."

"Someone might want to buy an early ticket. . . ."

"Hardly anyone ever does. Besides"—I force myself to say it—"there's always Austin."

"True."

"Also! You really want to see Elissa, don't you?"

"I guess . . ."

That's all I needed. In seconds, I'm dragging Jackson across the street to Taco Juan's. A guy's got to eat, right?

"Oh, hey," Elissa says when the bell over the door jingles and we step in.

Things about Elissa: She's pretty but not too pretty. She doesn't look fake. She tries to keep her hair neat, but it's so curly that's hard to do, and right now I want to go behind the counter and fix it. I hope Jackson doesn't want her to be a Rita Hayworth—you know, perfect every second of the day, glamorous. I hope he just likes her for her.

"We're here for ice-cream cones," I tell Elissa, taking full control of the situation. "Two scoops on waffle cones with extra sprinkles. I want chocolate-chocolate chunk and mint chunk. What flavors do you want, Jackson?"

Jackson is taking way too long to pick—I mean, seriously: pistachio, vanilla bean, mocha swirl, rocky road, strawberry, lemon-lime, chocolate this, chocolate that, just pick one—and before he makes up his mind, Elissa answers for him.

"I don't think Jackson really wants an ice-cream cone," she says.

"Yeah, sorry, Dani," he says. "But you should still get one."

"Why not?" I say. "It's perfectly normal to have ice cream for breakfast in the summer. It's like, you know, yogurt . . . just way better."

"He can't have ice cream," Elissa tells me. "He's lactose intolerant."

"Oh," I say. Just hearing her say it out loud, it's almost like proof of something.

Jackson shrugs. "It's true," he tells me. "I can't eat dairy."

There's an awkward silence as Elissa starts scooping and Jackson just stands there, watching. Also, notice how they're talking to me and not to each other.

I'm reminded of the times before the divorce, when my dad still lived at home and we'd all have dinner together. When we'd sit at the table and my mom and dad would barely say a word to each other, so Casey and I would have to talk for them.

We'd talk about the stupidest things. Favorite flavors of soda. Soccer. TV shows. YouTube videos. Teachers at school. That annoying girl who rides our bus.

It didn't matter what we said so long as we kept talking. And I guess I should have figured something was wrong by the way Mom would talk directly to me or Casey but never to Dad. And how we'd ask Dad a question and he'd sit there, rolling a meatball around on his plate, and we'd say, "Dad! Dad! Are you even listening? Dad!" And then at long last he'd look up from his meatball and see us and go, "Huh?"

But I didn't see anything wrong. I was too naive back then. I was only twelve. I know a lot more now.

I turn to Jackson. "Is it fatal?" I ask. "If you eat ice cream, I mean."

"What?" he says, laughing. "Of course not."

"But you can't have milk?"

"No," he says.

"Or cheese?"

"Nah. I get sick."

"Like how sick?"

"Just— You don't want the details, okay?"

"But it's not like you'd die," I say carefully, "if you had, I don't know . . . pizza."

I hold Jackson's eyes. I want to say there's a flicker of recognition there—like he knows who he's up against now: me. But no flicker. Not even a blink. He just says, "Nope."

Elissa's made herself busy building my waffle cone. She's also made an ice-cream-free sundae for Jackson: sprinkles, crushed Oreo, and nuts all mixed up in a waffle bowl. We take a table in the back, and Jackson and Elissa speak directly for the first time:

"So what time do you get off today?" Elissa asks him.

"Ten?" Jackson mumbles.

"At night? I thought you said you had the night off."

"I didn't say that."

"You did."

"You must've heard me wrong. I never get Monday nights off."

"Ooooo-kay."

"Don't be like that."

"Like what?"

"Like you're being. Right, Dani? Tell Elissa she shouldn't be like that."

I get a jolt from the sound of my name and spill a drop of ice cream on the table. "Oops," I say. I head off for the counter—away from them—to get a napkin. Once at the counter I take my sweet time pulling out a napkin from the dispenser. I wiggle and finesse it out, as if I want the smoothest, most wrinkle-free napkin ever in the history of Taco Juan's. As I do, Elissa and Jackson whisper, and I strain to hear them.

Elissa's mumbling. I think she says, "But you're never around when you say you're going to be around." Or else she says, "But you never wear brown when you say you're going to wear brown." Let's go with the first one.

To that, Jackson mutters under his breath and I catch the words "not true" and "you're exaggerating."

Elissa whispers something I can't hear except at the end, when she says, "Do you?"

Jackson answers her forcefully, and with a whole hidden meaning that's way over my head, *"Yes."*

I wonder what she asked him.

A few silent seconds pass, so I return with my napkin and clean up my mess.

They've completely stopped talking. Elissa picks out a chunk of Oreo from Jackson's bowl and eats it. Jackson chews up a walnut. Elissa cracks off an edge of the waffle bowl and places it absently on the table. Jackson flicks it off.

What's going on here, someone tell me, please!

That's when I notice his hand. He keeps shaking it out. And there's a purplish splotch on it, like he either smeared it in the raspberry sauce or he's got a bruise. Maybe it's from, oh, I don't know, *punching a hole in the wall when he said he didn't?*

"What happened to your hand, Jackson?" I say.

"Huh? Nothing," he says, standing up. "I should run. Gotta get the reel ready."

He walks off but then turns back. I figure he's about to say something to Elissa, something really cute and surely embarrassing that boyfriends say to girlfriends that I wouldn't have wanted him to say to any other girl in my presence before today.

(I once had a boyfriend, in seventh grade, for almost six days. He obviously didn't know how to be one because he'd say things like "Maybe I'll see you later at your locker." Or "Are you gonna sit with me at lunch or what?" That was pretty much it.)

But Jackson only says, to me and not to Elissa, "*The Big Sleep*—you seen it yet?"

I shake my head.

"Lauren Bacall and Bogie," he says. "You know who Bogie is, right?"

"Humphrey Bogart," I say.

He grins, like, *bravo!* Like this isn't the most obvious of movie-star questions he could have asked. Then he says, "See you there." And is gone.

Elissa finishes Jackson's leftover Oreo crumbs and dusts off her hands. "I should get back too," she says, and heads up front.

There's not a customer in the store—it's too early in the morning for anyone to want a burrito or ice cream, I guess—but Elissa looks alert behind the counter.

What just happened?

I head up front with the rest of my cone and lean against the glass case. I'm making hand-streaks across the fogged glass, drawing jungle animals, which means she'll have to wipe them all off with a rag before her boss sees, but she lets me do it.

"What's going on?" I say finally. "With you and Jackson, I mean."

I've just finished tracing out the shape of a Saharan elephant on the glass case. I decide to give it a little friend and begin tracing a giraffe.

Elissa shrugs. She tries her usual smile, but it doesn't stick. Then all of a sudden she lets out a breath and says, "I have no idea. You thought that was weird too, huh?"

"Yeah," I admit. "Like, *so* weird."

"I swear he said he had off on Monday nights. You believe me, right?"

I nod. I do believe her.

"It's not like he's the only projectionist who works at the Little Art," she says. "There's some old guy who comes in too, right?"

"Yeah," I say. "Larry."

"I know he said Monday," Elissa repeats. "And now he's acting like he never said it. It's like he's hiding something, don't you think?"

"What?" I say. "What could he be hiding? What do you think it is, what?"

(Think I sound nervous? That's 'cause I so am.)

Elissa lets out a heavy sigh. "I have absolutely no idea," she says.

I realize that she has no clue about the girl in the polka-dot tights, none. Elissa is blindfolded in the darkest part of the theater. And here I am, I could pull off that blindfold. I could hit the lights. I could open my mouth. I could . . .

So why don't I? I guess I just need to be sure.

I start tracing a new animal on the glass case. The animal has a long, lean body, and a tail, and sharp claws. It's a great big cat—a panther, maybe.

"Remember when you and Maya used to come here all the time and just hang out?" Elissa says.

It's such an abrupt change of subject—maybe she doesn't want to talk about Jackson anymore. Maybe she doesn't want to know.

"Yeah." I give the animal spots—it's now a leopard.

"You guys used to be in here every weekend, I swear," she says.

Maya's a sore subject. She hasn't called in more days than I'm going to count. I made at least three comments on her page online and I can't remember the last time she made a comment on mine.

And the thing is, she only moved to Poughkeepsie a few months ago. How can she have this whole other life in so short a time and I'm still moping around in mine?

"It was so sad that she had to move," Elissa continues. "Do you know I was at her house babysitting her brother I think the week before she left?"

"Yeah?" I say.

"She was so upset. She said she'd have to find a new best friend in her new school. She said she'd miss you so much."

"Yeah, but why?"

"Why? Because you two were so close. Of course she'd miss you."

"No, I mean why does she have to find a new best friend? *I* didn't."

"I don't know. I guess maybe it's lonely to be in a new place and not have someone to talk to?" She shakes her head. "It doesn't have to be a *best* friend," she adds. "Just a friend."

Is that a hint? Well, I'm not taking it.

What I'm going to do is go all Rita Hayworth in *Gilda*: I don't need anyone or anything. That's what I want people to think. I want to turn my shoulder and walk out of the room and not look back, no matter how desperate I am to keep looking.

"Whatever happened to Taylor?" Elissa says. Another change of subject.

"She's around. I saw her the other day. She broke one of my toes."

"She did what?"

"Joking."

"You two used to be in here all the time too, remember?"

"That's ancient history," I say.

I'm not sure where she's going with this. Is she trying to say there's no difference between Maya and Taylor? That I should just flit from one to the other like best friends grow on trees? Well, I know this is Shanosha, and we do have a massive amount of trees, but best friends are a once-in-forever kind of thing. You can't just forget them when they're gone.

Besides, just because Maya's down in Poughkeepsie doesn't mean she's vanished for good. She might be too busy to chat online, or send me a text, or leave me a message, or any other kind of human communication, but she still exists. I just wish she'd call sometime.

"Hey, Dani," Elissa says softly. I look up. She points down at the glass case, where a trail of chocolate has destroyed the giraffe. Not to mention the mudslide of ice cream that found its way to the front of my shirt. "You're dripping," she says.

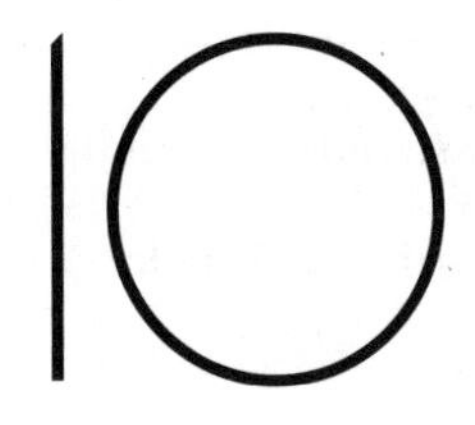

Glue Poisoning

I *stand in the street, covered in chocolate,* going over my options. The movie will be starting soon, but if I run home—almost ten minutes each way—I may miss the beginning. My mom's newspaper office is just one block away. She might have an extra shirt there that I can borrow. She also might give me a hard time about eating ice cream for breakfast. That's a chance I'll have to take.

When I walk in, my mom's preoccupied with some girl. They're talking all serious near the window, their backs to the room. I notice that my mom has her arm around the girl's shoulders. She's so up in this girl's business, she doesn't even notice her own flesh and blood standing here in dire need of attention, not to mention a clean shirt.

I clear my throat.

My mom turns around. "Danielle!" she says. She looks guilty. I don't get it until I take a closer look at the girl.

Taylor.

I think there's some unwritten rule that once you stop being friends with someone you can't hang with their mom. If not, there should be.

"Sorry," Taylor says to me. I wonder if she has any idea what she's apologizing for. She slips out from under my mom's arm and stands up. My mom stands beside her.

"Oh, Danielle, is that your new shirt?" my mom says, her eyes alighting at last on my reason for coming up to her office.

"Wow, what happened?" says Taylor.

"It's *chocolate*," I say.

"It sure is," Mom says.

My shirt, which happens to be bright yellow, a color that sets off chocolate really well, is obviously ruined. I want to get it off as soon as possible. But when I ask my mom if she has an extra shirt, she says she doesn't—I'll have to go back home to get one. And I just lost precious minutes by taking a detour up here to check.

"What are you doing eating ice cream this early anyway?" Mom says.

Quick, I need a diversion.

So I change the subject to my old standby—movies. "*The Big Sleep* is playing today," I say. "Bogie's in it, you know."

Mom doesn't look too impressed. I have a feeling she won't forget the ice cream.

"I have a shirt you could borrow," Taylor speaks up. "I was going to go tubing later and change into it after, but . . . You can have it if you want."

"Since when do you go tubing?" I say. The Taylor I knew didn't even like to get her hair wet, let alone dunk herself in the river and go hurtling down the muddy rapids.

"Since when do you like *Bogie*?" she challenges me.

I guess a lot has changed in the year we've been apart.

"You two should go tubing together!" my mom says.

"I am not going tubing," I say. But . . . "But I'll take your shirt," I tell Taylor.

She smiles and whips it out of her bag. It's black, which

is great. But on the front is a fuzzy iron-on of a tiger head. It's geeky beyond belief, and I can say that, even if I was the one drawing jungle animals on the ice-cream case just minutes before.

"Is there something wrong with it?" Taylor says.

"No . . ." I flat-out lie.

"Just tell me," Taylor says. "You don't like the tiger?"

"You know how I feel about iron-ons."

"Then wear it inside out."

"Good idea, I will," I say, and stomp off to the bathroom.

Inside, I change quickly and then stand very still to listen. I am positive they're talking about me. Just when I have my ear suctioned against the wood of the door, someone knocks in that exact spot and busts open my eardrum.

"Ow!" I yell involuntarily. "Who is it?"

"Your mother."

I open the door a crack.

"That wasn't very nice," she says quietly.

"I don't know what you're talking about."

"Let me in," she says. I roll my eyes and open the door so she can squeeze into the small bathroom with me. She closes the door behind her and then gives me this look. You know, the *look*.

"Taylor offered you the shirt off her back," she says. "You didn't have to insult her by saying you'd wear it inside out."

"She told me to!" I say.

My mom just shakes her head.

"Sorry," I mutter. Though, in my defense, the shirt was in Taylor's bag, not on her back. And also? I think I should get points for doing Taylor a favor and letting her know how lame her shirt is.

Mom does not agree. "You should tell Taylor you're sorry, not me. And . . ." Her eyes settle on the shirt I now have on inside out.

She doesn't have to say it. I quickly remove the shirt and put it on right side out. With that iron-on tiger head snarling out to the world.

The drama with the shirt almost made me forget what my mom was doing snuggling up to Taylor when I came in. "Why's she here anyway?" I ask.

"Actually, I wanted to talk to you about that," Mom says.

I lean up against the sink, waiting.

"She spent most of July at her grandma's house and now she's back. And the summer's so quiet . . . and she hasn't had much to do. . . . And so she came by to ask, well, if the newspaper needed an intern."

I wrinkle my nose. I've heard of interns. They work all day for free at jobs other people do for money. They don't get to sit around and watch movies whenever they want or eat ice cream whenever they want or hang out on rooftops pretending to get suntans. What a thing to volunteer for in the middle of summer. Taylor's become even weirder than I realized.

"Which gave me an idea," my mom says. "About what *you* could do with the rest of your summer."

I look at her without a single thought in my head. Nothing's coming. Really.

She claps her hands, then announces, "You could both be interns!"

Now I'm positive: My mom is not well. Mentally. She was haunted by water bottles and buried under boxes of tissues and now, when she's finally gotten herself together out in public, she's decided to force her only daughter to slave away making her photocopies and licking her stamps. I could get heatstroke, or glue poisoning.

"What do you think?" says the crazy woman otherwise known as my mother.

"You don't mean . . ." I start and can't finish. I point at

myself. Or, more directly, I point at the velvety tiger head, stabbing my thumb into its left eye, where my heart is.

She cannot seriously be saying I should spend the rest of my summer at the newspaper office. It's not like I could possibly learn anything here. We're not talking about a big-city paper. We're talking about a paper for a town with nothing happening and no one in it. Shanosha, New York: Look for it on a map. You'll find Albany, but it's south of that. You'll see Poughkeepsie, but it's north of that. On your map will be Kingston and then Woodstock, but it's west of them. Go too far west and you'll hit the state of Pennsylvania. So where is it? you'll ask. And to that I say: *Exactly.*

That's not to say my mom's job isn't important. It is. Even though *The Shanosha Scoop* reports on who's having a yard sale and whose dog ran away and here's her photo and *Look! We dressed her up as a princess for Halloween, have you seen her?* I'm proud of my mom for what she does. But that does not mean I want to do it.

"Mom," I say, "I've got better things to do." I open the door and slip out.

Taylor's waiting at a desk. Her smile falters when she sees me.

Mom follows me. "What things do you have to do?" she says.

"There are *things* going on right now"—I give Taylor a

once-over, decide she can't be trusted—"*things* I can't talk about here. Things about *people we know*."

"It could be fun," Mom says, ignoring what I just said. "We could find something you're interested in. For example, Taylor here wants to be a writer."

Taylor blushes, as if my mom said her dream in life was to be a rodeo clown or a gym teacher. Taylor used to be my best friend, sure, but I don't think I ever knew she officially wanted to *be* something. I guess that happened this past year too.

"So are you going to write stuff for the paper?" I ask Taylor.

She nods. She looks nervous, like I'll make fun of her. I have no idea where she'd get an idea like that.

"And?" I say. "What are you going to write about?"

So quietly I can barely hear she says, "Your mom said I could do a movie review."

"You're kidding," I say.

"No," she says, but it sounds like a question. Like she's asking me for permission.

As she should.

I've never seen Taylor in the Little Art, not once. She doesn't know the ins and outs of the self-serve popcorn machine. She doesn't know what seats not to sit on in the theater—and there are many. She doesn't know about Orson Welles or Humphrey Bogart or Ingrid Bergman or Rita Hayworth.

"Who's your favorite movie star?" I ask. It's a test.

Taylor blinks, considers. "I don't know. I guess I don't have one."

Test failed. I turn to my mom. "Mom, this is so not fair and you know it."

"Does this mean that you *do* want to be an intern?" my mom asks, a hint of a smile on her face, as if she planned it this way all along.

"Yeah, so do you want to do the movie review with me?" Taylor asks. "I was thinking we could watch whatever's playing at the Little Art and then write it at my house, you know, after. You could sleep over."

"I don't know. . . ." I say.

"That's a great idea!" my mom says.

I consider. Taylor's house is outside of town, up this winding dirt road back behind the elementary school. It's even more secluded than my house, and going there was fun when I was a kid, and made for some scary sleepovers, but there's something about staying at Taylor's house that freaks me out. It's her parents. Her perfectly nice, perfectly happy parents. All two of them.

"Maybe," I say, not meeting Taylor's eyes. "But I have to go. The movie's starting, and I told Jackson I'd be there."

"Okay," Taylor says. "I don't have to go tubing now. You're right, anyway, I don't even like tubing that much, I was just bored." She gathers up her things. She's going to follow me to the theater. "I think I want to watch the movie," she says.

"I guess I'll see you there," I say. And then I race out of the newspaper office, down the stairs, ditching her. There's something I need to catch, and it's not a movie. It's the liar projecting the movie.

I'm on to you, Jackson. Watch out.

11

Sorry, Wrong Number

S*o, way back a long time ago,* before phones came in pink and could fit in your pocket, they were fat and black and needed a whole table to stand on. I learned that this summer, from the movies.

Back then, if you wanted to make a call, you called the operator and she'd connect you. In the movie *Sorry, Wrong Number* the femme fatale, Barbara Stanwyck, is sick and stuck in bed. She's all alone, and has no one to talk to, so she keeps trying to reach someone, anyone, on the phone. But when the operator connects her, the lines cross and she overhears a whole other conversation instead. Two men are planning to kill someone that night. She just heard a big secret she wasn't supposed to—and you can't sit tight and do nothing after that, right?

Right?

I cross the street toward the Little Art. Unfortunately, Austin's the one at the ticket booth, and when he sees me he starts waving. He's not going to let me in without a ticket, I just know it. I sigh and skulk on over.

"Don't give me a hard time today," I tell him. "I'm not in the mood. You won't believe what my mom says I have to do."

"Fine," he says from behind the glass, "I won't give you a hard time." Then he adds, "Wait, you're not going away, right?" He looks a little freaked out.

"Going away where?"

"To your dad's, for the rest of the summer . . ."

The horror of these words cannot be measured. But what's weird is Austin's face as he waits for my response. It's like he really wants me to stay in Shanosha. Like he wouldn't know what to do with himself if I wasn't here.

"As if you'd miss me," I say.

For a second there, I see it clear: He *would* miss me.

He chops that thought down fast. "No, it'd be great," he

says. "I wouldn't have to police the theater looking for loiterers, which means I could actually do my job."

"One, you don't really have a job. And two, that's what you think I'm doing? Loitering?"

"I don't know, Dani, when's the last time you actually paid for a ticket?" He searches my face. "Can't remember, can you? I could report you to the authorities, you know. You could be banned from the premises if I said the word."

"Then say the word."

He does not say a word.

"Anyway," I continue, "you won't believe what my mom said. She wants me to help at the paper for the rest of the summer. She wants me to be—get this—an *intern*."

"Cool," he says.

So not the right answer. Before I can blast him, we're interrupted by the sharp squawk of his walkie-talkie. He jumps, like he does every time that thing goes off. You'd think he'd be used to it by now.

"Hey, cuz. You there?" comes a staticky voice through the walkie. Jackson.

I am not here, I mouth through the glass. Let's hope Austin can read lips. I want to listen in without Jackson knowing.

"Affirmative," Austin says into the walkie.

"Dude, are you there or not?" Jackson's voice squawks.

"That's what I said, Jackson," Austin says, rolling his eyes at me. But I won't give him the satisfaction of responding because, hello? He said "affirmative" instead of just saying "yes."

"Hey, did anyone call me before?" Jackson asks.

"No, why?" Austin says.

"Some girl?"

"I said no. Why?"

Ask who, I mouth. *Ask her name.*

Either Austin is deficient in all forms of lip-reading or he's ignoring me on purpose, because he doesn't ask.

"No reason," says Jackson. "Later."

Then there's another high-pitched squeal, and I cover my ears. Austin fumbles for a long second that's sure to cause me permanent hearing loss, then at last switches the walkie off.

"He's gone dark," Austin says. "He keeps doing that. I'm glad he agreed to use the walkies, but he's really supposed to say 'over and out' first. How many times do I have to tell him that?"

"Whatever," I say.

I reach into my pocket, find some crumpled bills, and slide them in through the hole in the ticket window.

Austin stares at my money. "What's that?" he says.

"What do you think it is? It's money. For a ticket."

He stares at it for a beat too long, so I snatch it back. "I guess that means I get a freebie today. Thanks!" I push through the doors and take my place in Theater 1.

The Big Sleep stars Lauren Bacall as the femme fatale. She's not Rita Hayworth, but she's pretty okay. This is the film where Bogie fell in love with her in real life, so I'm trying to see it. What made him pay attention. When it happened. How.

Love and like and all the rest make no sense to me. Sometimes you like someone and they don't like you back—does that make it any less real? Take Elissa and Jackson—they both like each other, so there shouldn't be a problem. And don't get me started on Mom and Dad.

In *The Big Sleep* someone's blackmailing Lauren Bacall's sister. Slowly, as I watch, something dawns on me. The visit Jackson blamed on pizza delivery. The phone calls that got him so raging mad he punched a hole in the wall. Secrets kept, things not said. You know, if this were a noir movie, you'd think he was being blackmailed.

Let's say someone—some girl—has information on Jackson

he doesn't want to get out. She's threatening him with it, and he's trying to keep her quiet. What could it be?

I turn in my seat to take a peek at the projection booth. There's Jackson, all alone up there, as he should be.

I also catch sight of Taylor sitting on the other side of the theater, in an aisle seat. I didn't see her there until now.

Back to the movie. Lauren Bacall's telling the private eye played by Humphrey Bogart that he forgot one thing: "Me," she says.

"What's wrong with you?" says Bogie.

"Nothing *you* can't fix," says Lauren Bacall.

Cue the romantic music. Go in tight for a soft-focus close-up. You know they're about to kiss here, and even so I take the opportunity to turn around and check the projection booth once more. Now Jackson isn't in there. No one is.

Just then I catch sight of Jackson slipping out the lobby door and into the light. What's up with that?

I climb up the dark aisle and crack the door, peeking out into the bright lobby. I see the tail of Jackson's jacket, just a flash of it as he turns the corner into the hallway. Then I watch his legs climb the stairs toward Ms. Greenway's office. When he's safely up there, and most definitely can't see me, I follow.

I tuck myself into a spot in the shadows. The passage here cuts to the left in a sharp, blind corner. If I stand with my back to the wall, I can hear him up in her office. Taking a seat on her wheelie chair. Picking up the phone on her desk. Dialing.

And as he does, I realize something. I'm pretty sure that phone is on the same line as the phone in the hallway. The phone I happen to be standing next to.

I pick up, all sneakylike, keeping the mouthpiece covered with my hand.

I hear ringing. One ring, two rings, three. On the fourth she answers.

"Finally," she says. "Take your sweet time calling me back, why don't you."

A few things about this girl's voice: It's deep for a girl—I bet she got stuck with the altos in chorus. There's no foreign accent, so she's definitely from around here. Oh, and she sounds mad. Very mad.

"Well?" she says. "Aren't you going to give me one of your patented excuses? Like your aunt made you paint the theater. Or she sent you out to restock the soda machine. Or you fell off your bike and forgot my phone number. So what is it this time?"

Jackson answers her back all whiny: "My cell gets sucky

reception in here. I've told you that. . . . And you can't keep calling the theater. My aunt doesn't like it, okay?"

At this blatant lie some sound comes out of my mouth, like a click of my tongue, something involuntary. The next thing you know Jackson's saying, "Did you hear that?" And the girl's saying, "Hear what?" And Jackson says, "I don't know, like a click or something." And then they're both dead silent, listening.

I can't hang up now—they'd hear. So I do the only thing I can: hold my breath and play statue. I'm standing here in the dark, my weight more on one foot than the other, anxious Jackson will come out to the stairwell and see me. I look down to make sure the shadows cover me. And they do—almost. All except for my big toe.

If Jackson steps out of the office to look down the stairs, he will see, around the corner and in the light, the incriminating stub of my big toe. It's sticking out of my flip-flop. I painted my toenails bright blue. There's no way he could miss it.

The girl starts talking again. "I don't hear anything. So like I was saying, you could at least call me back, like on your break or something."

Jackson sighs.

The girl sighs.

I take it they have this conversation a lot.

"Anyway," the girl continues, "I don't believe you're really coming over tonight. If it's anything like last time . . ."

"I'll catch the bus like I said, okay? It won't be like last time."

I remember then that he told Elissa he was working tonight. He didn't say anything about catching any bus.

"Last time you never showed up."

"I'll show up."

"I don't believe you."

"Believe whatever you want, Bella. You'll see, tonight."

Bella! Nichole was right. I hate that she was right.

"Oh, I *will* see you tonight," the girl—Bella—says. "I'll make sure of it."

"What's that supposed to mean?"

"That means I'm not counting on you to catch the bus like last time. I'm coming to Shanosha. I'll borrow my brother's car again. What time do you get off?"

"Late."

"How late?"

"Uh, seven thirty."

"That's not late!"

"I mean eight thirty. I forgot."

She lets out another sigh. "I'll be there at nine."

"Listen," Jackson says. His voice sharpens. "You can't come here, not to the theater, not to the house."

"Why not?"

"My aunt, I told you. She's really strict."

Lie.

"She won't let me have a girlfriend while I'm living here."

Lie.

"She makes me work all the time. It's like I'm on call 24/7."

Lie.

"So I have to meet you somewhere else," he says. "Okay?"

"Where, then?"

"Remember that playground with the castle? There. I'll meet you there."

"By the seesaws?" she asks.

"Yeah," he says.

I hear Jackson hang up the phone, so I hang up the phone. I look with longing at the door to Theater 1. I'd have to cross the hallway to get to it. I'd have to walk right in front of the stairway. There's no way I'd make it in time, no way.

So I shrink deeper into the shadows. I make myself as small as I can manage, sucking in my gut and all my toes.

He bounds down the stairs and past the hallway where I'm standing without even a look in my direction. In seconds, he's back inside Theater 1, the door swung shut behind him, like he'd never even come out.

A whole entire minute passes, but I can't move. I wonder if he'll notice I'm not sitting in the audience like I was before. Why didn't I think of that? Before I can figure out my next move, the phone on the wall rings.

Recklessly, I shoot out my hand and answer it. "Little Art. Can I help you?"

"Hi, uh, who's this?" says a girl's voice. *Bella's* voice.

"Who's *this*?" I shoot back.

"Sorry, I think I have the wrong number." And she hangs up.

Austin stomps out of the ticket booth to glare at me. "Who said you could answer the phone?" He glances up the stairway. Jackson left the light on. "Were you in my mom's office? I promised her nothing would happen while she's out. I *promised*."

"Nothing happened. I just came out for popcorn and the phone rang and I picked it up and it was that girl again, like you said."

"So now you admit I was right."

"Just go sell your tickets."

I head for the popcorn station and fill up a bag. This, I now realize, will be my alibi. If Jackson asks where I was, I'll just say I wanted popcorn. *What?* I'll say. *You didn't see me at the popcorn table? I was there the whole time.*

When I push through the doors of Theater 1, Jackson's standing in the aisle, gazing up at the end credits.

"Hey, D," he says. "Where'd you go?"

"Popcorn," I say, shaking the bag. "I was sitting there watching the movie and I was thinking I really want popcorn, so that's what I did. I was out there, I swear, getting popcorn." I give the bag another shake.

"You like popcorn," he says. "I get it."

People are so much smoother with lies in noir movies. I've got to practice.

"Popcorn is so great," I say. And I smile. And I hold out the bag. And I actually say, "Want some?"

Why am I being so nice to him?

"Yeah, sure," he says, scooping up a handful.

Why am I not confronting him when he's standing right here?

"So tigers, huh?" Oh, great. Now he's making fun of the shirt.

"Don't say it."

"It's very retro," he says. "I like it." There is no way to know if he's lying.

The credits roll off into nothingness. The movie's undeniably over. The sound goes quiet so all I can hear are his teeth, chewing that popcorn to bits. If I'm going to say something, right now would be the time. Only, I begin to wonder. Like, if he knows. Like, if he's aware I was listening in on his phone call. If he does know, he'll blackmail me into not telling. It'll be just like in *The Big Sleep* except I don't know what will happen because I didn't see the end.

"That's strange," he says as he chews.

"What?" I say, too quickly, too loudly. "What's strange?"

"There aren't any toppings on this popcorn. It's totally plain. That's not like you."

He's right. When's the last time I got a bag of popcorn at the Little Art with *absolutely nothing* on it? Never, that's when.

"Sometimes people can surprise you," I say.

And then, just to prove it, I take a handful of plain nonbuttered, nonsalted, noncinnamoned or -paprika'd or -anything'd popcorn, and shove it in my mouth. I mash it up and swallow like this is the way I wanted it and how could he think otherwise. Like *yum*.

Taylor drifts up the aisle, hovering. I'd forgotten she was here. She waves a reporter's notebook at me that's filled up with scribbles. "Did you like the movie, Dani? I took notes so we can do the review."

"Yeah, Dani," Jackson says, "so *The Big Sleep*, what'd you think?"

Did I like the movie, did I like the movie, did I like the movie . . . ?

I'm thinking.

Then I remember an important detail: the playground where he said he'd meet Bella tonight . . . it's the one with a castle in it.

There aren't too many playgrounds in Shanosha. What do we need playgrounds for when we have the woods? There's the playground at the rec field. It has a set of swings and a pit of sand to dig around in, no castle I can think of. There's the playground in the park by the river, if you'd call a basketball court with one hoop and a rusted jungle gym a playground. And then—jackpot—there's the playground at Shanosha Elementary School.

Why didn't I think of it sooner? I went to that school from kindergarten through sixth grade. In it, there's a wooden replica of a castle that forms a tunnel maze of slides. I haven't played on that thing in years. Only the little kids use it—or so I thought.

If only I could get to that playground tonight . . .

You do realize the solution is standing right here, waving a stack of scribbles in my face. Someone I know lives just down the road from Shanosha Elementary.

"Dani," Taylor says, "did you like the movie or not?"

They're both standing here, waiting for my answer.

"Definitely," I say, with feeling. "I can't wait to go to your house tonight and write that review."

12

Secret at the Seesaws

T*aylor's halfway through her movie review,* the one I'm supposed to be writing with her, when she looks up, sees me sprawled out on her beanbag chair staring up at her bedroom ceiling, and asks, "Why are you even here?"

I hear the question, but I don't exactly *hear* it. Just like I'm staring up at her ceiling, but I'm not seeing her actual ceiling.

My mind is racing. In a movie, we'd be reaching the part where the audience is reminded of everything that came before. Important clues will flash on-screen to make sure no one's forgotten.

So what I'm seeing on Taylor's ceiling is a conveyer belt of things. This thing. And that thing. And the next thing. Revolving all around me.

Elissa. Jackson. Polka dots. Pepperoni. Ice cream, ice cream, more ice cream.

A girl by the name of Bella. A wall with a hole in it. A phone that's ringing. A walkie-talkie with Austin talking into it. (Wait, get Austin off my conveyor belt!)

"Dani! I thought you wanted to do this with me."

I tear my eyes away from my movie-on-the-ceiling to find her, elbows out and back straight, sitting at her computer like school's already started and this is homework.

"You don't really want to write that review now, do you?" I ask her.

"Yeah," she says, "sort of. But you don't."

"We should take a break," I say. "Maybe go for a walk?"

Taylor pinches up her mouth. I know that look. Just because you haven't been friends with someone in a while doesn't mean you don't recognize all their faces from back when you hung out. People change, faces not so much. I know Taylor's mad face. Her tired face. Her excited face. Her leave-me-alone face.

This face here—pinchy mouth, flinchy eyes—means she

wants to say something she's not sure she should. Chances are she won't say it. She'll say something else instead. Watch:

"Okay," she says. "We can take a walk, if you want." I wonder what she really wanted to tell me.

But it doesn't matter, because it's nearing nine o'clock and it's super important we leave her bedroom, like, right away and head out for the school playground. She doesn't need to know exactly where the walk will take us.

She gets up and puts her computer to sleep. "It's getting dark out," she says. "We can take a walk in the backyard, if that's what you mean."

"Your parents will let us go down the road and back," I say. "If we ask." She knows this is true. It's not like we haven't done it before.

Her house is at the end of the road in a cul-de-sac—if you want to pretend this is the suburbs and call it that, but this is upstate and there are barely any other houses around, so we should just call it what it is and say dead end.

You could be out on Taylor's road all night and see no one. If you spot a car, it's like a shooting star. You point at it and follow its light until it streaks away.

There's no reason why we can't take a walk down her road

and back (with a detour to the elementary school, *shh*), and she knows it. It's not like we're babies who don't know the way home.

So she sighs, and the pinched look fades, and without any more argument she agrees to it. The Taylor I remember used to have more of an opinion about things, but for some reason, tonight, she's letting me have my way.

I follow her out of her room and down the stairs so she can ask her parents. Her mom and dad are in the living room, sitting close together on the couch, watching some movie. Taylor's dad works at the elementary school. He's a bit on the short side, his beard a little scruffy. Taylor's mom owns the jewelry store in town. She's a tad glamorous and a lot tall, like someone from the city and not here. I have no clue why they're so happy together. But look at them:

Taylor's mom leans her head on Taylor's dad's shoulder.

Taylor's dad has his hand on Taylor's mom's knee.

They're sharing a bag of chips, and when we walk in, both their hands are in there together, mingling at the greasy bottom of the bag, like they don't care whose fingers belong to who.

Taylor also has a little sister, practically a baby, who's asleep upstairs. When they're all together, eating dinner at the dining room table, talking and chewing and stuff, they're exactly what you'd expect a family to be.

"Could we take a walk?" Taylor asks her parents. "Just down the road and back?"

"You can if you bring your cell phone," Taylor's mom says.

"Of course," Taylor says. To add to the perfect world where her family exists, they somehow live on this patch of mountainside that miraculously gets cell-phone reception. Seriously. I'm standing in her living room and I get all five bars.

"And bring flashlights," her dad says. "It's getting dark."

"Sure!" Taylor says.

"And please take out the trash," her mom adds.

"No problem!" says Taylor, like she loves doing her chores all the time.

"Come here," her mom says. And this is where they hug, the three of them, so this is where I turn around and stare at the wall.

It ends quickly and Taylor and I head toward the mudroom to grab flashlights. Just as I leave the room, I hear Taylor's dad calling my name so I step back in.

"Good to see you here, Dani," he says. "It's been a while." He's looking hard at me, taking in everything and anything that has changed in the year seventh grade came and went. I guess my hair's different, to my chin now instead of long. Oh, and I have the bangs. If that says something about the new me, I'm not sure what it is.

They seem to be waiting for some kind of response, so I say, "Yeah."

"We missed having you around," her dad says.

"So did Taylor," her mom says.

"Thanks," I say, and I leave the room quickly, before the conversation can continue, before they ask me why. Because sometimes I have no idea why.

Taylor and I take out the trash and then walk down her road, flashlights in hand. We follow her dead end to where it stops and stand there, idling. Her flashlight beam wobbles all over the pavement. I keep mine still.

"So I guess we go back now?" Taylor says.

"I have an idea," I say, like it just came to me. I peek at the time on my cell phone—8:53 p.m. Sweet. "Let's go on the swings. At the school."

The face she gives me is the one where she suspects something isn't right, but I head off before she can ask what that might be.

We reach the school from the north side, looking down a low

hill at the back of the playground. I lead Taylor to a shaded area beside a jungle gym and duck down, take a look around. Then I see them, at the seesaws. Jackson's standing in the dim light, leaning on his bike. The girl—Bella—is on the bottom of the seesaw, but she can't make it go, because there's no one at the top.

"I thought you wanted to go on the swings," Taylor says. And then she sees what I see and adds, "Hey, isn't that Jackson from the movie theater?"

"Yup," I say. *"Shhh."*

She turns very quiet and doesn't protest when we sneak over to hide behind a slide. The castle built up over the slide—big enough to fit more than a few kids inside—casts a deep, dark shadow. When we're covered by that shadow, plastered up against the castle wall, it's nearly impossible for anyone to see us. This is the ideal place from which to spy.

From here, we have a clear view of the seesaws. We're too far away to hear anything, but I'm not sure if we should move any closer. Between the slides and the seesaws is a wide-open expanse of sandboxes, no good cover, nothing to hide us.

Bella has her back to me. In the night, I can't tell if she's wearing polka dots, but I'm positive it's the same girl I saw sneaking out the fire door. It couldn't be anyone else.

Taylor tugs on my arm. I whisper, *"What?"*

"That's not Elissa."

"Yeah, I know."

"Oh," she says, eyes widening. "Oh."

I nod.

"Wow," she says. "Who is she?"

"Her name's Bella."

"Okay, but *who* is she?"

"I don't know yet. That's why I'm here." I'm not going to say she's Jackson's girlfriend. In my mind, Jackson can have only one girlfriend and that title falls to Elissa. So I don't know what to call Bella. She's the other woman. The femme fatale. The one we have to hate—I think.

I point toward the last slide before the sandboxes, the one farthest away. Under it is a triangle of deep black shadow. Once there, we'd be golden. There's no way anyone could see us in there, and yet we'd be able to hear absolutely everything.

I'm trying to indicate this to Taylor with just my eyes and a few hand gestures, but she's not getting it.

"What?" she whispers.

I point, I sign the concept of running with two swirling fingers in the palm of my hand, but then I stop with a jolt. I hear something. And it's not coming from the seesaws—it's coming from the other side of the playground, behind us.

I can tell Taylor heard it too, because she freezes. Her eyes go wide. "What's that?" she hisses.

"Someone must've followed us."

"Who?"

"Your mom? Your dad?"

She shakes her head.

"One of your neighbors?"

"I don't have neighbors, you know that."

All this takes place in whispers. We're afraid to move, but we do, slowly, in the smallest of increments, turning our heads toward the sound.

We hear:

Absolutely nothing. Whatever it was, it stopped.

We see only the dark night, which is suddenly so much darker than it was five minutes ago. It's like the sky is playing tricks on us, luring us out here and getting us caught in something we shouldn't have been in. We're out alone. We're being followed. Taylor's parents don't know where we are. Hey, what kind of movie is this anyway?

The noise starts up again—shuffling, whirring, tap-tap-

tapping—heading straight for us. Taylor looks even more freaked out than I feel. Whatever's pounding in my chest is pounding five times faster in her chest, I can see it. And even though I push my panic down, even though I tell myself it's probably just a raccoon, I guess Taylor can't do that. Or else she's really scared of raccoons. Because she hisses, "Run!" And then she takes off, flinging herself into the darkness, before I can stop her.

13

The Big Chase

T*aylor's off.* She's running for the swings. I take one last look at the seesaws, figuring Jackson and Bella must've heard us, but apparently they're far too busy to pay us any attention. They're doing things I don't even want to see, don't even want to know. I find myself looking, blushing, then I pull my eyes away.

I have to go after Taylor.

And I can't forget that we're not alone. Whoever's followed us here weighs way too much to be a raccoon. And I don't want to think about bears.

It's officially dark now, too dark to see. I don't want to call attention to myself by switching on my flashlight, so when I hear another crunch of approaching steps, that same low whirring noise, that same faint tap-tap-tap, I lose control and start in the direction of the swings too.

First, I walk fast to the jungle gym. Whirs and taps and crunches of gravel follow.

I cross through the jungle gym and speed to a nearby tree.

A pause. Then a tap. Then a whir. It's coming closer.

I take a deep breath and make a run for it. At the monkey bars, the whirring turns to hissing, but I don't go back. I dive into the deep, dark chasm of night that stands between the monkey bars and the first set of swings where I think Taylor must be.

Those few moments I'm running through the dark last longer than can even be possible. I feel like I could run forever, never stop, that I could leap over that swing set, hit the road and whatever's beyond the road, bound up the mountain and over to whatever small nothing of a town can be found on the other side.

What really happens is I reach the swing set in barely a heartbeat. Taylor's here. I bend over, heaving, trying to catch my breath.

Out there in the dark, the hissing is louder now. Something that sounds a lot like spinning wheels runs over gravel. A scream bubbles up in my throat—I just might blow our cover and let it out—when, clear as can be, I hear someone whisper: "Dani . . . ? Taylor . . . ? Where are you?"

I realize Taylor is holding my hand. Or else I'm holding Taylor's hand. It's not clear who grabbed whose hand first.

She speaks up, braver than I am, I guess. "Who's there?" She doesn't sound scared any longer, she sounds fierce. Protective. I'm glad she's here.

"It's me," says the voice. And it comes closer, and the whirs whir faster, and the taps tap louder, and then here he is, right in front of us, Austin, wandering around in the dark with his dirt bike. "Why'd you guys run?" he says. "It's just me."

I let out a breath. I don't want him to know how scared I was—for just that one second, just the one—but I can't speak at first.

Austin's laughing. "Who'd you think it was?"

Now Taylor's laughing. "We didn't know!" she says.

And me? No way, no how am I laughing.

I swear, I can't go anywhere without running into Austin. He won't leave me in peace at the movie theater. He won't let me be when I'm walking down the street. Now he's following me to sleepovers? Chasing me through the night?

"What are you doing here?" I snap.

He stops laughing. "I rode here," he says. "On my bike."

"I didn't ask how you got here. I asked what you're *doing* here."

My eyes are starting to adjust and I can see Austin now, so obviously and completely Austin I should have known it couldn't have been anyone else.

He waves in the far-off direction of the seesaws. "Jackson snuck out," he says. "He rode his bike, so I followed on mine."

"That's far," Taylor says.

"Yeah, and now it's dark. So I don't know how I'll get back."

"Listen," I tell Austin, "we're here on a mission. There's something we've got to do. So just leave us be, okay?"

"I'm not here on a mission," Taylor says. "I didn't even know we were coming here. She tricked me, if you want to know the truth."

"She does things like that," Austin says. I feel them in the dark, judging me.

"Fine," I say. "You guys stay here, I'm going in for a picture."

"A picture of what?" Austin says.

"Of them," I say. I point to the two figures by the seesaws.

They're still there, doing whatever it is they're doing. But if we wait any longer, they won't be. And then I won't have any proof.

"For what?" Austin asks.

"Yeah, for what?" Taylor says.

I throw up my hands. I don't have time to explain it. I take a step away from the swings, back toward the monkey bars.

"Are you certifiably insane?" Austin says.

I don't answer that.

"You're not going back there alone," Taylor says. "We'll go with you."

"We will?" Austin says.

"Yeah," says Taylor. "We will. C'mon."

Taylor keeps surprising me. But I lead the way, my phone out and ready to snap a picture. Soon we're in the shadow of the castle, scoping out the seesaws.

Jackson may have been kissing that girl earlier, but now he's not doing anything of the sort. Now they're just talking. Actually it's more like arguing.

"I don't believe you!" Bella says. I can't see her face, but her voice carries out over the playground like she doesn't care who might hear. "If I find out you're—" She has trouble getting it out. "I'll, I'll—" She mumbles something I don't catch.

"I'm not," Jackson says. "I swear."

Bella doesn't respond.

"Do you believe me or not?" Jackson asks. He uses a little-boy voice, like he's the innocent one here. I can't imagine any girl believing anyone who uses that voice. Rita Hayworth would hear that voice and she'd cut him down to size before he got out his next breath.

Bella turns around. She just looks at him. Thanks to the streetlight nearby, I'm able to see the quickest of glimpses of her face: her mouth, only that. Her lips are painted dark, like any femme fatale's would be. I bet she's deadly beautiful. I bet she's unforgettable. She has to be, if she's the one with Jackson.

Her mouth stays closed, not uttering a word, the expression on her lips impossible to read.

Jackson repeats his question: "I said, do you believe me?"

She answers at last. "Yeah." Disappointing me.

I wonder what it was she was supposed to believe. Then I know. I figure it out. If she's the femme fatale, the other woman, the cheat, then she knows all about Elissa and wants her out of the picture. She's telling Jackson to break up with Elissa, and he's saying he will.

I must do what I came to do. I pull out my phone and get ready to take the photo.

"She's pretty," Taylor whispers.

"She's evil," I say.

"I don't know," Austin butts in to say.

"What, you don't know if she's evil or if she's pretty?"

"I mean . . . are you sure she's evil?" Austin says. "Maybe she doesn't know he already has a girlfriend."

Yeah. Right.

I point my phone at the seesaws. It's dark, so I'm going to have to use the flash. Once that goes off, they'll notice. Once the photo is taken we'll have to turn tail and run. But it's worth it.

I hold out the phone. I try to keep it steady, except my hand's making it shake for some reason, my hand, or my arm, or my whole entire body is shaking so much that the picture shakes. It's just normal stakeout jitters, I tell myself. I take a breath. I prop up the phone on the edge of the castle so it'll stay still. I hold it tight and aim it at the seesaws. I wait for just the right moment, press the button, and—

At the exact moment I snap the photo, a shriek of noise cuts through the playground. Someone is singing. It's a girl, a girl standing really, really close to me, belting out a pop song.

I don't know if I got a good picture or not. I didn't see the flash go off.

I turn in horror to find Taylor holding her own cell phone, which is lit up and blasting her ringtone. *Someone* didn't think to set her phone on silent.

Taylor freaks and shuts the ringer off before it can do any more damage. As if. Jackson and Bella would have had to be on the other side of the river not to hear that.

"Who's there?" Jackson yells.

In seconds, we hit the ground, crouching on the asphalt beneath the castle, breathing heavy. I look at Taylor. She looks at me. Austin looks at me. I look at Austin. We have no idea what to do.

"We heard you," Jackson yells. "We know you're there."

Taylor whispers she's sorry. She takes hold of the castle wall and pulls herself up. But I grab her shirt and pull her back down. I try to stand. It should be me who goes, not her.

But before either Taylor or I can go, Austin does something strange. He stands. Then he turns and whispers something to us. Finally he steps out into the light. He wheels his bike over to the seesaws, calling out to his cousin. He takes the rap for us and he never looks back.

Taylor and I sneak away as Jackson starts making fun of Austin about his girly ringtone. We slip out of the playground from the north side and head back to Taylor's house without anyone spotting us.

What did Austin tell us before he turned himself in? He said, "Just go. You guys were never here."

Caller ID shows that the call was from Taylor's dad. We race back, flashlights in spasms all over the road like we're trying to run on a trampoline. When we reach her house, we find her parents standing in the mudroom.

There they are, waiting in the narrow entryway that's crammed full of rain boots and umbrellas and way too many pairs of flip-flops for a family of four. It's clear her parents want to stop us before we even remove our shoes. For a moment I wonder if they're going to let us inside the house at all.

"Where have you been?" Taylor's dad says. "We called three times."

Sure enough, there are now two more missed calls flashing on Taylor's phone. With her phone on silent, we didn't hear them.

"I drove down the cul-de-sac and back," Taylor's mom

says. "You said you were taking a walk down the road. Where were you?"

"We were, uh . . ." Taylor says, flailing for the words. And then, as if we've just come back from robbing the town bank and she wants it known it wasn't her idea, she steals a glance right at me.

"We took a detour," I answer for her. "It wasn't far."

"A detour to where?" Taylor's dad says.

I'm not sure what the right answer should be, so now I look at Taylor.

"A detour to where, Taylor?" Taylor's mom asks.

"The playground," Taylor admits. "To take pictures."

I can't believe she said that! Now I have to step in to bend her truth more in the direction of a reasonable lie.

"Of the slides," I shoot out randomly. "For an art project."

"At night?" Taylor's dad says.

"Yes," I say. "It's an *art* project."

I realize that may have come out more sarcastic than it should have. Plus, it occurs to me that Taylor's dad is not my dad, and Taylor's mom is not my mom, and maybe they won't put up with what my parents put up with.

Taylor's mom and dad are both appraising me at the same time. With two parents determining the depth and weight of your lies, it's more than a little overwhelming. I feel sorry for Taylor then, with her two parents and her nice house with perfect cell-phone reception. I feel sorry that she breaks so easily, that she doesn't know when to stay quiet, that she thought now, of all moments, was a time for the truth.

"Go call your mother, Danielle," Taylor's mom says. "She might want to come pick you up."

"Now?" I ask, and then when I see they're not letting up, I say, "Okay."

My mom answers after five long rings. "Wuh?" she mumbles.

"Mom?" I'm in Taylor's dark kitchen, where her family can't hear.

"Mmmmm, huh?"

"Mom, are you sleeping?"

"Yeah." A pause as she sighs. Another pause as she fumbles with the phone. "What time is it?"

"I don't know, maybe ten. Where are you?"

"On the couch," she says.

She sniffles then and this is when I wonder if she's been crying. She was left alone in the house for a night and what she did is curl up on the couch and cry herself to sleep. I can't leave her for one night.

"Did you eat?" I ask softly.

She sighs again. Sniffles again. Tells me to hang on, and I wait while she blows her nose. Then she comes back and says, "I had crackers. Is that why you're calling, to make sure I ate? I'm fine, really. I want you to have fun at your sleepover. I'll see you at the paper tomorrow, all right?"

"Yeah, okay."

"Havin' a good time with Taylor?"

"Uh-huh." And here is where I could slip in that I'm having such a good time with Taylor that I got her in trouble and her parents want someone to come pick me up, but I don't say that. I don't know how to, what with my mom the way she is right now. So I let her say good night, and I say good night, and she hangs up the phone, and I guess Taylor's stuck with me for the rest of the night.

I leave the kitchen and find Taylor and her parents in their den. "She can't come get me now," I say. "Sorry."

Sometimes I wonder if I carry my whole entire story written all across my face. If everyone can see it just by looking at me. Because Taylor's parents don't ask anything else of me. They say it's fine if I stay the night after all, and with one last glance at each other they send us up to bed.

***

"Why'd you do that?" Taylor asks once we're up in her room. She sounds mad.

"Do what?"

"Go spy on Jackson. . . . What does it matter to you if he's cheating or not?"

"Because it's Elissa," I say. "Because," I continue, sputtering. "Because he lies!"

"But you just lied, downstairs, about the art project."

This quiets me a moment.

"He's way too old for you," she says, wrinkling her nose.

"What?" I say, too fast, too soon. "Don't be disgusting."

"You know what?" she says. "You don't have to explain. I get it."

"You do?"

"Yeah." I realize she's not going to say it out loud—*you're mad at your dad, so you're taking it out on Jackson*—because she knows I'll deny it to the moon if I have to.

I make myself busy by digging around in my bag for my toothbrush.

"So if you want to go home now you can, you know," Taylor says. "My dad would drive you."

I find the toothbrush and pull it out. "I don't want to go home," I say.

"Because now I know why you came, so . . . so you don't have to stay, okay?"

I look up at her. She's standing rail straight in the middle of the room, but her nerves show through on her face like the palest skin on the underside of your arm can show all your blood vessels. She's afraid of what I might say.

"I don't want to go home," I tell her. "Really."

I want to say more. To tell her about the ring my dad gave Cheryl, about October, but I sort of can't. The words to explain it aren't here.

"What *happened*?" she says.

"He's obviously seeing that girl behind Elissa's back. But now I have a photo so—" I stop talking. I don't think Taylor meant what happened with Jackson just now. I think she meant what happened between her and me.

"It doesn't matter," she says. "So you're staying?"

I nod.

There's more that could happen here, confessions and apologies and never-agains that could keep us awake all night, till the sun comes up and it's a new day. We could decide we're friends again, officially—if we want to be. But there's no movie script for this scene, so I'm not sure what should come next.

"Can I use your toothpaste?" I ask.

"You know where it is," she says.

And that's enough until morning.

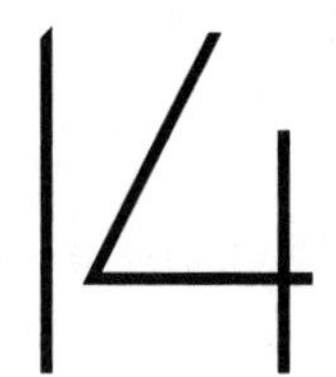

Blackmailed

I*'ve been trapped in the newspaper office* for hours already, and there are still hours more to go until lunch. Here I am, helping Taylor with this movie review, wasting away in my windowless cell while the rest of the world goes on without me.

Okay, fine: The room does have windows. Only, I'm sitting at a desk so far away from them I can't see even one tree. And I'm dying of thirst, and all my mom has here is water. And I want to confront Jackson. I want to check on Elissa. I want to *do something*. This internship is eating away at my life.

This is when the escape plan comes to me. "I have low blood sugar," I tell Taylor. "I need juice. I'm going down to the Corner Cupboard to get some."

"I'll go with you," she says.

"It'll only take a minute," I lie. "I'll be right back," I add, lying again.

She looks at me for a long moment—she knows—but all she says is "Okay."

My mom, for her part, just asks if I could grab her a cranberry.

So this is how I end up out on the street, free at last. First stop: Taco Juan's. But Elissa's boss says she's on break. So I set my sights on the Little Art. In the blink of an eye I'm inside the theater, crossing the velvet rope and stepping into Theater 1. It's between shows, so the lights are on and the movie screen is blank—but the door to the projection booth is open and from in there I hear something.

Voices.

One belongs to Austin. "I swear, I won't tell anyone, not anybody, I promise," he whines. The door to the projection booth is open only a crack, so I can't see for myself, but I'm willing to bet he is either crying, or *thisclose* to it, which is something I don't want to see, not now and not ever.

The other voice belongs to Jackson. "I can't believe you followed me," he says. "You little snitch. How am I supposed to believe you'll keep your mouth shut?"

"I *swear*," Austin says. "I swear on Monster. I swear on Henry the Eighth." (Monster is his cat. Henry the Eighth is the last of his cat's kittens, the one they haven't been successful in giving away yet.)

"You swear you were there by yourself? No one else was with you?"

"It was just me," Austin says. "I was there alone."

"Okay," Jackson says, "if you say so, okay." I'm not sure if he's trying to convince himself or if he really believes Austin.

"Can I go now?" Austin squeaks.

"One more thing," Jackson says. "Swear to me you won't tell Dani."

"Dani? Why would I tell her?"

"If you tell her she'll tell Elissa, you know it, so swear to me. Say you swear."

"I swear."

"You swear what?"

"I swear I won't tell Dani."

"Or . . ."

"Or what?"

"Or *I* will," Jackson says in this low, menacing voice.

A cloud of silence descends and swallows up the projection booth. Nothing's coming out, not a word, not a mutter, not one more squeak. It's like the sound cut off at the high point of a movie. Something essential is about to be let loose and *wham*—

Some slob trips over the cord and the speaker goes out.

I hear nothing. With the door cracked like this, I see nothing.

Wait. They don't know I'm here, do they?

Then Austin speaks up, so I guess not. "Okay," he says at last. "I won't tell her."

And then it hits me, how little sense that whole exchange just made. Jackson doesn't want Austin to tell me, so if Austin does tell me then Jackson will tell me too?

But I'll already know. *Austin would've told me.*

Hit pause and try to figure out *that* logic.

"Can I go now?" Austin says.

"Yeah, go," Jackson says.

And then, before I can get a handle on the situation—namely that Austin is now leaving the projection booth, and if he takes the door on the side where I'm standing, he'll step down and turn and see (um, hi) me—I realize I've got to get out of here.

The camera slips into slow motion, or time does, at least. My foot is lifting off the ground and then my knee is lifting and then my whole leg. My body pushes forward like trying to find footing in Marshmallow Fluff—and as this is happening time moves so slowly you could read a page in your social studies homework, go to the kitchen, make a Toaster Strudel, come back, eat it, realize you got crumbs all over your social studies homework, shake the homework over the garbage disposal to get the crumbs off, go back to the den, take a nap, finish your homework, paint your nails, and then at last my foot would have touched ground and I would have taken one step.

That's how slow of slow motion I mean.

I'm one inch closer to the door when Austin emerges and sees me. With a flying leap—I didn't know Austin had it in him—he grabs me and pushes me out through the exit into the lobby. We land, panting for breath, at the popcorn stand.

"Quick! Get busy," Austin hisses, and we launch into a serious operation involving one bag of day-old popcorn, three shakes of cinnamon, four of cayenne, a flurry of coconut flakes, and Parmesan galore, until Jackson comes out and sees us.

"You're here early again, Dani," he says, looking at me sideways. By that I mean he's looking at me and he's also *looking* at me. He's trying to see if I'll stop shaking the Parmesan and break.

"I wanted popcorn for breakfast," I lie. "Austin just came out, and I was like, Austin, don't *you* want popcorn for breakfast? And he was like, Totally. And I was like, So help me make it! So that's what we're doing now."

"Butter," Austin says.

"What?" I say, breaking out from my sea of lies.

"We forgot the butter." He gets out a gelatinous mound of something that may be butter—I'm not positive. He pours it with abandon over the concoction of popcorn, and it slides there, shifting around, until it settles, like liquid soap. The what-we-assume-is-butter sinks down into the lower reaches of the popcorn slowly, like ear wax coming alive and spreading down your body to your feet. I glance away, try not to gag.

"So how is it?" Jackson asks. A look of amusement is perched on his face. Also a look of challenge.

Austin peeks down at the waxy, spotty concoction with alarm. "I don't know yet."

Jackson stands there, waiting.

I do the brave thing, the thing one of us has to do to get out of this: I eat some popcorn. Then I go, "It's different." My voice rises a few notches as I say that. The word *different* is really all I can manage for the roadkill I just put in my mouth.

Austin's eyes bug out. Then he takes some too. And puts it in his mouth. Chews it. Turns paler than a turnip. Seems about to choke. But, to his credit, does not.

"It looks disgusting," Jackson says cheerfully. Then he heads out of the lobby.

As soon as Jackson's out of sight, Austin starts spitting.

I cry out for water.

We're in great agony over what we've just swallowed for a good five minutes before we can even speak to each other.

"I heard you guys talking," I say at last.

"I figured," he says.

"Why'd you lie?"

He shrugs.

"So what did he say about Bella? I got there too late, and I didn't hear everything."

"I can't say."

I stop. Step back. Go, *Huh?*

"He made me promise not to say." Austin mumbles these words while staring with deep concentration at the black-painted floorboards, unable to look up and meet my eyes.

"Did he blackmail you or something?" I ask. At first I'm joking. I've got noir movies on the brain, that's all. Except now I see Austin twitch, see his eyes hop and jitter across the black expanse of the floor to get away from me.

So it *is* true. I push him to say more. "What will happen if you tell me? Will Jackson like . . . *do* something to you?"

My mind reels out possibilities: baseball bat to the knee, pee in the soup, snake in the bed. No, Jackson wouldn't do any of those things, not to his own cousin (except, maybe, the snake). More likely Jackson has something on Austin, a deep, dark, dirty secret. They're family—they've got to know things about each other that others don't. Like, does Austin suck his thumb when he sleeps? Was he born with a tail and the doctors chopped it off before his parents brought him home? It could be anything.

Instead of answering, Austin pretends to be very interested in housecleaning. He bends down to pick up a lone popcorn kernel from off the floor. Who knows how long it's been there, maybe since last summer, the summer of slapstick comedy. A funnier, happier time, I've heard.

"Well?" I say.

"Well, what?" he says back.

We've come to a roadblock. I'm getting nothing out of Austin today.

"I should go," I say. Before I make it out the door, a hand grabs me.

"Listen, just don't tell him you know, okay?" Panic in his face, a grip stronger than expected on my arm.

"Okay . . ." I say, snatching my arm back.

It's clear Jackson does have a secret on Austin . . . but what? Something that would land him in juvie, maybe, like those eighth-graders who defaced the school auditorium and were never seen again and I can't even remember their names now. It could be something just as shocking but without the shaving cream or Silly String. Or it could be even worse. Wow, maybe Austin did something really bad, like ran someone over with his bike.

"What happened, Austin? What does he know? You can tell me."

There's a beat as he considers how much to say. A long, gaping, auditorium-wide beat. But then he just shakes his head.

"Fine, don't tell me. And don't freak out—I won't tell Jackson."

"Thanks," he mumbles. He seems about to say something

else. It's about the hit-and-run, I'm thinking, it's about the cover-up. But all he says is, "I didn't see you come in. Did you buy a ticket today?"

I give the door a great big slam as I stomp out to the street.

I'm on the sidewalk, heading back for the newspaper office, when my cell phone decides to start working again. I swear, the thing's possessed. Now I get the following text message:

U FORGOT UR JUICE

The text is from a number I don't recognize. No name shows up in my Caller ID. But it's this area code, so it's someone from the county, it could be someone from this very town. And if that someone knows I didn't get juice, they're nearby. Watching . . .

I look around wildly.

Then my eyes shoot up—straight into the windows of the newspaper office. I catch sight of Taylor, her shadow looking down on me, almost ominous. I guess she saw me go into the Little Art instead of the Corner Cupboard. I guess she knows I had other, more important things to do than write that review with her.

Last we were friends, she didn't have a cell phone. I guess I never programmed in her new number.

I text back: K THNX

Let's pretend she's not mad at me, that she was just sending me a helpful reminder. I wave to her and run over to the Corner Cupboard to get some juice, an orange for me, and for my mom a cranberry. At the last second, I grab one for Taylor, too: a cranberry-raspberry twist.

15

Seeing Spots

I*t's a new day and today's plan is to confront Jackson* at long last, to trap and tangle him in his own lies. I can do it without even having to tell him what I saw.

A good detective, one trained in the art of catching criminals, is like a walking, talking lie detector. The way to get a confession is to be tough—hard as nails, they call it. Just an hour alone in a room with the perp, lightbulb aimed square at his face, and all will be revealed.

Thirsty? No water for you—not till you tell me everything.

Sleepy? You'll stay awake till you tell me what I want to hear.

I know you did it. We have witnesses. You can't hide it from me, so spill.

At least, that's the kind of junk they say in the movies. And when your perp looks like he's about to crack, you just keep throwing questions at him, blinding him with the hot, bright light until he can barely remember his own name.

Where were you on the night of July thirtieth?

At home, you say? No alibi, you say? What size shoe do you wear, an eight-and-a-half? Aha! Gotcha.

Soon enough, the perp starts talking. You don't even need to match his shoeprint. Soon, he's signing the confession, and you're walking out saying you saved the day.

I guess.

I mean, maybe all that would work if the crime were something more obvious, something that would send you to jail. With a thing as delicate as this, when someone's heart is on the line, and she's someone you know and like, such as your old babysitter, a girl who's calmed you after you had a coat-zombie-in-the-closet nightmare (yes, *again*), who's bandaged up your scraped knee, then you have to be more careful.

Besides, Jackson might not respond to me shoving a table lamp in his face.

Just imagine if my mom had someone who cared this much about digging up the truth back when my dad was sneaking around. It might not have been too late. Things could have been fixed, and turned good again, and my parents might still be married today.

I'm not deluding myself. It's possible. Admit it's *possible*.

So the plan is simple: Wait for Jackson to come downstairs, tackle him at the door, and then pull out, strand by incriminating strand, the truth. All I need is a little help from Austin.

And for Taylor to look the other way when I skip out on the internship again. And for my mom not to ask where I am. And for it not to be raining because I forgot an umbrella and I'm getting soaked.

Let me set the scene:

Back behind the Little Art movie theater, I'm tucked beneath the exterior stairwell leading up to the second-floor apartment where Ms. Greenway, Austin, and Jackson live. Rain's coming down, but the sun's still out somewhere, if you bother searching around in the sky for it. The mountains are dead gray. The puddles are getting wider, threatening to reach my toes. Jackson's red bike is locked up to the railing, so I know he's not out riding it. I'm hiding here, waiting for him to come down.

I think Jackson is the first person in the history of Shanosha to use a padlock to secure his bike in his own backyard. It's like the city people who drive through here on the way to their resort cabins, the ones who think the Catskills are pretty, not agonizingly dull. They stop for ten minutes to get a cone at Taco Juan's and actually *lock their car doors* while they do it, like they think we mountain people are all robbers and carjackers. Jackson's just like them.

That's the interesting thing about liars: Not only can they not be trusted, they don't trust anyone else.

So I'm waiting here under the stairs. Jackson doesn't start work until four in the afternoon, so I guess he's not up yet. I stand here, dripping. I stand here for a long time.

Meanwhile, Austin's upstairs in the apartment, poised to give me a signal any minute now. The mission I talked him into was simple: Keep an eye on Jackson's whereabouts and report back when he gets his lazy butt out of bed.

No sign of movement and it's, like, two in the afternoon. My cell phone's blinking in and out, so I keep losing track of time, but if I need to be contacted I have the walkie-talkie as a backup—Austin's idea, obviously.

The minutes tick past. The rain falls on the stairwell, pattering over my head. The sky has gone dim, tricking me into thinking it's later than it is. Jackson sure sleeps late. . . .

Suddenly the walkie chirps. "Home base to Eagle Three," the thing squawks. "Do you copy? Over."

I push the button to talk: "What did you just call me?"

"You didn't tell me a code name so I made one up. Over."

"Stop saying over."

"You're *supposed* to say over. Over."

"Austin, do you have something to tell me or what?"

No response.

"Austin!"

A shower of static almost as loud as the rain.

Fine. I say it: "Over."

Having now heard what he wanted, he says, "Jackson's not here. I don't know what happened, but he left. Sorry, Dani."

I give up on the walkie-talkie nonsense and stomp up the stairs. I pound on the door until Austin answers.

"What do you mean he's not here!" I shout to be heard over the rain. Next I expect thunder to crash, lightning to strobe out the sky. How did he lose Jackson while they live in the same place? I don't know how that's even possible.

I should've been paying more attention, because my question

is answered by what Austin's wearing. A bathrobe. Plus a towel wrapped like a turban over his thick head.

"Please tell me you weren't just in the shower," I say.

"Not the shower," he says, "the bath." He shrugs. "Look—you're getting rained on. Do you want to come in?"

"You were supposed to be watching out for Jackson and you *took a bath*?"

"You really should come in."

But I can't get over it. This is what I'm working with, someone who thinks it's perfectly okay to bathe during a stakeout. A bath, while on duty. A bath, in the middle of the day.

A bath!

My disgust must be visible on my face because Austin starts going off on me. "What do you want me to do, Dani? I said I'd help because you wouldn't take no for an answer. You never do. You always want everyone to be there when you want them there, and you're never there for anyone else. Ask Taylor. You're the most selfish person I've ever met in my whole life."

I stand there, the rain—heavier now than before—running down my face.

"Aren't you going to say something?" he says. "Like make fun of me because I have a towel on my head? Get it over with already."

I sigh. "I am not," I insist.

He doesn't argue, but he doesn't take back what he said either. "I'm going to lend you an umbrella, and you're going to take it, okay?"

Now I'm the one not to argue. I take the umbrella that's offered and spread it open over my dripping head.

"I don't know where he went," Austin says. "He was sleeping in his room when I got in the bath and when I got out he was gone."

"But I was down here the whole time. There's no way he came out this door."

"He could've gone downstairs the other way—straight into the theater."

"There's another way down?"

"Yeah," he says. Then, almost sheepishly, "Didn't you know that?"

"No!" I shriek.

So you know, I'm blocking out what he said before. I pretended I didn't hear what he said while he said it, and I'll continue to pretend until I can figure out why he'd think such a thing. Me . . . selfish?

Jackson is selfish. My dad is selfish. Cheryl is selfish. Nichole is selfish. Casey is selfish. Maya is selfish. Even Taylor is selfish because she wants me up there in the boring newspaper office when I have better things to do. And Austin is the most selfish of all, for thinking this was the time to take a bath.

Selfish? Me? Not on your life.

I could say all this to Austin now. I could defend myself. But that's when I see it: a flash of something dark pink down in the street. Dark pink—with polka dots.

I fly off the stairs, not even bothering to say bye to Austin, though I should thank him later for the umbrella because it helps me sail to the ground without breaking a foot.

I might have been looking for Jackson, and he may have slipped out of sight before I could find out where he was headed, but I now have what's called a lead. I've got to follow it.

The last time I saw polka dots, they happened to be attached to the legs of that girl, Bella. She must be here in town to meet Jackson.

But when I reach the sidewalk, the polka dots are gone, lost in the rain. She must have went that way . . . or this way . . . or this other. She must've gone south, or west, or east. She could be anywhere, in any part of town.

Then I see the spots again. They're definitely dark pink

polka dots. Magenta, you'd call them. And they're attached to what appears to be an umbrella.

It almost does look like a movie—for real, this time.

In the distance, through the falling rain, it's hard to see the girl who's holding the umbrella, but I do see where she's taking it. I spy the flight of the umbrella veer off the sidewalk and down along the bike path to the river. So I follow.

As I hustle quietly through the rain I see flashes of what could happen once I catch her—and I don't think that's lightning. Flash: I race up to her and reach out an arm under the umbrella, grabbing her by the shoulder.

Flash: She stops, knowing she's caught.

Flash: Slowly she turns and I see her face up close for the first time. She's not as pretty as Elissa, and even if she is I would never say so. She says, *What do you want from me?* I say, *For you to leave Jackson alone.* She says, *Okay.* And then, *Aren't you Dani? He talks about you all the time, you know.* I didn't know, but now I do. Then she says, *I'm so sorry I tried to take him from you.* Wait. No. *Elissa.* She says Elissa. And then she vanishes forever, leaving town in a flurry of polka dots that get washed away in the rain.

Flash. Actually, maybe that is lightning.

I'm down on the path, trying to be as stealthy as possible,

which is difficult when your sneakers have no treads and are slippery to walk in when it rains and send you sliding almost three whole feet down the muddy slope and as you go you make a tiny sound like, "Eeeeeee!" And when you look up, you see two people staring.

Jackson and the girl with the umbrella. Only, the girl with the umbrella is a girl you already know, a girl you've seen hundreds of times before, a girl who's known you for so long she may or may not have witnessed you wet the bed.

"Oh, hi, Elissa," I say. "Hi, Jackson."

"Dani, *what* are you doing down here?" Elissa says.

"I . . ." Nothing comes.

"Are you following us?" Jackson says.

"Where are you going?" It's not an admission of guilt, just a simple question.

"The gazebo," Elissa says, pointing at the wooden gazebo on the shore. It's a little covered shelter out of the rain. But she doesn't ask me to go with them even though if I stand out here for much longer I could get struck by lightning and electrocuted.

The Elissa I know is missing from under that umbrella. She's not smiling her usual smile. She's not happy to see me. I hate to say it, but she mostly looks annoyed.

"We're gonna go," she says, taking Jackson's hand. "See you later?"

"Later," Jackson says. His umbrella is plain black, forming a dark shadow over his eyes, which is very convenient for him, don't you think?

"Wait!" I shout, once Elissa and Jackson are halfway to the gazebo. "I *was* following you," I admit. "Elissa, I really need to talk to you."

"What about?" she says. She is still holding his hand.

"It's personal," I say, eyeing Jackson. I wait and she's still standing there holding on to his hand. "Girl stuff," I add.

Now, Elissa may have the day off and want to spend it hanging out in a mildewy gazebo with her boyfriend, but deep down she's more than a girl with a day off and a boyfriend to spend it with. At heart, where she can't ever deny it, she is still my babysitter. That is a bond you just cannot break.

"Wait for me inside," she tells Jackson, pointing at the gazebo. "I'll be right there." When he's out of earshot, she says, "What happened? Did you just get your, um . . ." She looks uncomfortable.

"No! That was like a whole year ago!" I can't believe she thinks I'd chase her down to talk about something like *that*.

"Then what?"

"Where'd you get that umbrella? I've never seen you with it before."

She shrugs. "I dunno . . . the mall?"

"Oh," I say. I'm having a hard time finding the right way to say this.

She heaves a breath and lets it out, loud. "Dani, what are you doing here? I mean, for real. Is this how you're spending the summer, stalking people? It's creepy."

I take a step back, careful not to slip in the mud. "I'm not trying to be creepy," I say. "I'm trying to make sure you don't get hurt. Besides, I didn't think I was stalking *you*—I thought it was someone else. Like I said, I've never seen you with that umbrella."

"If you like the umbrella so much, you can have it," she says. She closes it up and I stand there shocked for a few long seconds until I realize it's stopped raining.

"Summer storm," she says, "comes and goes. Now, who did you think you were stalking and why did you think I'd get hurt?"

I lean closer. I can tell that Jackson is trying his best to eavesdrop from over in the gazebo. He's not watching us, but his head is inclined our way, ears peeled, listening.

"Some girl," I say as quietly as I can. "And because."

She doesn't get it. "I can barely hear you," she says.

"A girl," I say, eyes wide. "A *girl*."

"What are you talking about?" she says far louder than she should.

"I saw Jackson with another girl," I blurt out.

"I don't believe you."

"I swear. And I have proof." She eyes me warily as I pull out my phone.

"What are you doing, who are you calling?" she says. She has the strangest look on her face, full of panic and on high alert, like not only does she know something's about to happen, she knows exactly what.

I flip open my phone and start looking for the picture. Yes, *the* picture. The one I took in the playground, the one with Jackson and Bella on the seesaws, the one Elissa desperately needs to see.

"Elissa!" Jackson calls. "Are you coming or what?"

"Elissa, just wait a second, it's here," I say.

Her face has turned to cold, gray stone. "This isn't funny, Dani," she says. "I'll see you later, okay?" And then she's running over to the gazebo—she's left me her polka-dot umbrella even though it could start raining again any second, and she's gone to him, to Jackson. She's picked him over me.

I see him standing there, watching me. But when she reaches him, he looks away, like he couldn't care less what I know.

Elissa grabs his hand and they sit down on the bench inside the gazebo, in the shade, where they know I can't see.

16

Don't Trust the Tomato Soup

T*aylor was supposed to keep my mom from* knowing where I was. *Tell her anything you want,* I instructed Taylor, *just cover for me, and I'll be in later.*

Of course, waiting for Jackson to roll out of bed took way longer than expected, not to mention my detour to the gazebo. I was supposed to be in an hour late, but it's been at least three hours.

I sneak up the stairs to the newspaper office, lugging two more umbrellas than I had this morning, and walk smack into Taylor, who's pacing by the entrance.

"Where have you been!" she says.

"You know, *out*," I tell her. "I got a lead. I had to follow it."

"A lead on what?"

"On Jackson and that girl, Bella—only it turned out not to be Bella, it was Elissa." I fill her in on the details. "But Elissa doesn't believe me. And Jackson . . ."

"Wow," Taylor says. "Jackson acts like he'll never be caught."

"I know."

"Like he's invincible."

"I know."

"And by the time he moves back home at the end of the summer it'll be too late and no one will ever know what he did."

"I *know*."

She shrugs, this helpless gesture like, *Oh, well, that's life.*

I don't know what life she spends her time living in, but the one I'm in doesn't sit back and let things like that happen. Not anymore.

"I'm going to do something about it," I say. I have a whole speech planned out.

Only, before I get a word into the speech, Taylor's like, "But why? Why does it have to be you who does something? What about Elissa's friends, what about—"

"Because I should have told my mom," I say. "About the tomato soup."

Taylor looks beyond baffled, but I stop all talk about it when I see my mom. "You just got here and you're already getting lunch?" Mom says.

"Lunch?" I say. "I, uh . . ." I grind to a halt and glance at Taylor.

"It was rainy out," she finishes for me. "Dani was saying it's the perfect day for soup."

My mom looks from one of us to the other, like she doesn't believe it. "It's hot out," she says. "Are you sure you want soup?"

"Yeah, you're right," I say. "It's way too hot. Ice cream would be better."

"You can't have ice cream for lunch," my mom says, being a mom. Then she remembers I'm also her intern and turns all business. "Danielle, you know we're on deadline here. So I take it you got it while you were out for so long?"

Taylor must have told my mom I was so late because I was looking for something for the paper. But what? "Did I get it . . ." I pat the side pocket of my jeans. "I did. It's in here!" I announce.

My mom looks curiously at my pocket. "Really?" she says.

Taylor jumps in—she keeps doing that. "The picture, yeah. She downloaded it first and then e-mailed and printed it out. Just in case."

A picture? Of what?

My mom shakes her head as if she's used to me doing stranger things, then asks, "How's the ad page coming, Taylor?"

"Great!" she says.

"Good. We just got one more ad—can you fit this in?" She hands Taylor a piece of paper that says MIDNIGHT MOVIE in giant letters like a big marquee. I grab it from her and take a closer look. The Little Art is starting a new event every Saturday night through the end of August, a Midnight Movie, and for the first week they're showing *The Lady from Shanghai*, starring none other than Rita Hayworth.

"Jackson's been wanting to have a Midnight Movie for forever," I say, because I know about these things. "But Ms. Greenway kept saying no." I don't tell them this, but I wonder if he made the first one a Rita Hayworth movie because of me. Like it's his way of communicating something to me, something between just the two of us, and I'm confused all over again, forgetting I'm supposed to hate him now.

My mom waves at the Midnight Movie ad. "I had to call the

theater to be sure there wasn't a typo." She points to the spot on the ad that says MIDNIGHT MOVIE, EVERY SATURDAY 10:15 P.M.

"Why would they have a Midnight Movie at ten fifteen?" Taylor asks.

"That's what I asked," my mom says, "but they assured me it's correct. I guess 'Midnight Movie' sounds better than 'Ten-fifteen Movie.'" She smiles at me.

"I'm so there," I say. I glance at Taylor. "We should do a movie review."

"We?" Taylor says.

"Yeah," I say. "I can go this Saturday, right, Mom?"

"I don't know. It's pretty late. . . ." she says.

"It's for the paper," I say. "It's important."

"We'll see," she says cryptically. Then she goes back to her desk across the room, leaving Taylor and me alone to deal with the ad page.

"What picture was I supposed to get?" I ask quickly.

"Of the library," she says. "For the bake-sale story. I already took the picture this morning on my way here, but that's what I said you were doing."

"Good one," I say.

"I can't believe I lied for you," Taylor says. Then she peers across the room to be sure my mom's not listening. Some other guy who works at the paper—the designer or the art director or something—doesn't seem to be eavesdropping either. "What were you talking about before? What about tomato soup?"

"Let's go somewhere," I say. "You know . . . to talk. Privately."

"What for?"

She doesn't get it. I'm about to tell her something I've never told anyone. Not Maya, who was supposed to be my best friend. Not Casey, my own flesh-and-blood brother. And especially not my mom.

"C'mon," I say, and pull her out of the main office down the hallway, where things are quieter. I've been coming to the *Shanosha Scoop* offices since I was a kid—I know every place to hide out, every out-of-the-way corner.

"But I have the ad page to finish!" Taylor protests.

I also know that, here, deadlines are relative. The ad page isn't life or death. But what I'm about to say feels like it is.

Taylor backs away, though, when she sees where I'm taking her.

"That's a *closet*," she says.

"It's the old photography darkroom, back from before the paper used digital cameras. It's not a closet." I pull her in and close the door behind us.

"It sort of smells in here," she says. "And also—where's the light?"

I guess the room does sort of smell—thanks to all the chemicals they needed to print the photos, there's a faint, lingering stink like rotten eggs. Also, since the paper stopped using the darkroom they took out the orange safety lights, so the room really *is* dark. Even the windows are covered up by black shades. Taylor's probably thinking I'm some kind of freak for forcing her in here. So I push aside one of the shades to let a little light in.

With some light shining, I see the room is smaller than I remembered. There's just a counter and an old sink, nowhere to sit. Taylor hops from one foot to the other, impatient.

"I really, really, really have to do the ad page . . . ," she says. "Your mom asked me to. What's so important you had to tell me right this second?"

But I can't just jump into it. I need to make sure she understands first. "Ever seen *Double Indemnity*?"

She narrows her eyes. "Is that another noir movie?"

"Yeah, it's, like, one of the most famous noir movies."

"And . . . ?"

Double Indemnity—I never did get what an indemnity was,

double or otherwise, so I just watched it for the femme fatale. I try to bring it to life for Taylor.

"Okay, so there's this whole scene with the femme fatale and the guy she wants to run off with. And they're, like, plotting to get rid of her husband, and did I tell you the femme fatale is Barbara Stanwyck? You know who she is, right?"

"I have no idea," Taylor says. "Just tell me what this has to do with your mom."

"Fine." So I tell her. I tell her everything.

First, of course, I describe the movie in great detail. Barbara Stanwyck has to meet the guy so they can talk, but she has to keep it secret, right? He can't come to her house, or her husband will suspect, so they have to meet in public, somewhere no one would look twice. They choose a grocery store. There's a scene where they stand whispering in the aisle, pretending to shop, and all the while plotting a murder.

Taylor's eyes go wide at this, but I set her straight.

"I saw my dad's girlfriend before she was his girlfriend," I say. And I lean in. "In *a grocery store.*"

"Yeah?" she says, like it's no big deal.

"I mean, I saw them. Together. I think they met there on purpose—and they didn't think I'd figure it out."

She looks uncomfortable. "Your mom doesn't know about this?" she says.

I shake my head no.

Now I set the scene from real life—another grocery store, and this one way bigger than the one in *Double Indemnity*. The one in real life was a monster grocery store, the kind where you can buy anything you've ever needed, every fruit or vegetable or type of cracker to put your cheese on, rubbery upstate sushi, even socks. My dad wanted to go there for some reason, even though it's about forty minutes away off the thruway. He said he wanted to "stock up" on stuff, and then, maybe to look less guilty, he let me tag along.

So there we were, in the mother of all grocery stores, Dad and me together, food shopping. We were pushing the big cart around the aisles when I galloped off to grab some cereal. I was betting on the fact that he'd let me get Cocoa Pebbles, which Mom never would, when I came back to find him in Aisle 9, near the soup cans, talking to some woman.

I didn't know who she was. She was pretty, and blond, and she was standing real close to my dad, having what seemed to be a serious conversation. I noticed my dad was holding a Campbell's soup can: tomato. She had some other, chunkier, option—chicken, I think, with rice.

I wouldn't have thought it was too strange if my dad didn't do what he did next. He saw me coming and froze. He glanced at the can of tomato soup in his hand, and I swear he tried to hide it behind his back. "Hey there, Dani," he practically shouted.

The woman next to him jumped into motion. She bolted over to the shelf, putting the chicken-and-rice back and grabbing a pork-and-beans instead. And then my dad raced the cart out of the soup aisle and waved at me to follow.

That's it.

Taylor waits for me to reveal something else. Something more sinister than a grocery aisle, probably. But to me that's the worst of it—the ordinary place where it happened. The unsuspecting victim (me) happily wandering around with the box of Cocoa Pebbles, all while the bad guy (Dad) made plans to run off to the other side of the river with a stranger. Hey, maybe I'm not the only one who's seen *Double Indemnity.*

I've spilled all this to Taylor, there in the tiny darkroom, and then I add, "And he's marrying her now. Cheryl. My dad gave her a ring."

"Oh," Taylor says. *"Oh."*

And for some reason she doesn't have to say anything else.

I know she gets it, she really gets it. I can tell by the look on her face.

Suddenly there's a knock on the door. We open it and bright light steals in.

"What are you two doing in here?" my mom says.

"We were talking," I say. "Sorry."

"Taylor," my mom says. She does not look happy. "The ad page?"

"I'm on it," Taylor says guiltily. She rushes out, leaving me alone with my mom.

"You're not taking this seriously, are you?" my mom says.

"We are," I insist. Then I add a spot of truth, "Taylor is."

"It doesn't look like it," she says. And then she leaves me in the darkroom.

I hang back a minute longer, even though it really does stink in here. I'm thinking how there are some things you need to know—and some things you don't. And all at once I'm relieved, like really and truly relieved, that I did the right thing and never told my mom. Only, it makes me wonder . . . is there anything someone's not telling *me*?

17

Master Detective

T*aylor's hard at work on the ad page when I say,* "Listen, I have to do something on the other computer, okay? I'll be right back."

She doesn't protest, so I take all the time I need. I've decided to do a bit of detective work. Things are far easier for the private eye nowadays. We've got access to a handy little thing noir detectives never had back in the day: the Internet.

I realize there's an easy way to get the dirt on this Bella girl, to find out who she is, not to mention exactly what she is to

Jackson. Nichole said she was friends with Bella, so, logically, they're probably friends online, too. It's worth checking out.

While I'm online, my mom gets a phone call. I see her eyeing me from across the room as she talks. I ignore her, though—because I just found Nichole's page. There she is, for anyone to find, first-name last-name, her blond, pointy face warping my screen.

I found Nichole, but I can't see her page or her list of friends until she's my friend. So here's the question: How badly do I want this? Will I—*can* I—add her as a "friend"?

My mouse hovers over the add-friend button, unable to click.

"Danielle, what are you doing over there?" my mom calls.

"Research," I call back—and this is no lie.

"Researching what?"

"Bake sales." That is most definitely a lie.

"Fine. Just come over here when you're done."

It's now or never. So I close my eyes and I grip the mouse in my shaking hand and I give it one quick click.

Friend Request Sent, I read, and with that, I have died a little inside.

When I go over to my mom's desk, she's sitting there all serious, a drawn look on her face. I hop to attention, wondering who was on the phone . . . my dad?

"Are you okay?" I ask worriedly.

"*I'm* okay," she says. "Why, do I not look okay?"

"You never look okay," I say, then regret it.

She looks down at her hands. "Take a seat, Danielle."

I pull up a chair.

"I need you to be honest with me, Dani."

"Of course."

"Very, very honest."

"I will be," I assure her.

"You don't want to be here, do you?"

I assume she means Shanosha. And while I do wish I lived somewhere else, what's the alternative, outer space? "Yeah, sure I want to be here," I say.

"That doesn't sound too convincing. What about your friend Taylor?" Across the room, Taylor's so engrossed in the ad page I doubt she's even trying to listen in.

"What about her?"

"She said she wanted to be here—she asked me to do this—but I see the two of you goofing off and I don't know. . . ."

Oh. Mom means do I want to be here at the newspaper, and the answer to that is a definite no. But Taylor wouldn't say the same thing.

"She's not goofing off," I tell my mom. "Really. It's my fault, not Taylor's."

"I know you weren't out working earlier. And Taylor said you were."

"Taylor's just being a good friend, Mom. She's, like . . . really loyal or whatever."

"She always was." Mom is looking hard at me now—she wants this to sink in and make me a better person, I bet, someone who never makes even one tiny mistake or gets bored with her friends and thinks maybe there's something better around the next corner. Like I can take back how I dissed Taylor all those months ago. Like she'd forgive something like that. Like I should even hope it's possible.

Only, Mom doesn't say any of this. She takes a big breath and tells me, "As I said, Danielle, I know you weren't working before, no matter what your friend said on your behalf. I know you were out spying on Elissa."

"Wait, *what?*"

"Elissa called to tell me. She said you're trying to break her up with her boyfriend. Isn't that the boy who works at the theater? Jackson?"

She says his name with emphasis, and this is when I realize

that she knows. How I feel about him. Felt. Never to ever feel again. My mom's always known.

I stare into my hands as my face turns colors and reveals all. Nothing more needs to be said.

My mom continues. "Please, Dani, don't tell me that's why you're trying to break them up."

"No!" I shriek. "It's because he's cheating," I confess before I can stop myself. "Elissa doesn't know." I'm shocked Elissa would rat on me to my mom, but in a way I guess now I'm ratting on her.

"You think her boyfriend's cheating on her so you're trying to break them up?"

"I don't *think* he's cheating, I *know* he's cheating."

"Dani, I know why you're really doing this and it has to stop."

"But—"

"I told you it has to stop. Your father is marrying Cheryl. Face it. I know it's happening, you know it's happening, and there's nothing either of us can do about it, okay?" She stops short and I expect her to make a dive for the tissues, but she doesn't move. She doesn't even sniffle. "I know this summer's been hard on you. . . . And this internship certainly isn't helping." She pauses. I think she's done. I figure we're about to hug now. Then she surprises me by saying this: "I'm sorry, sweetheart, but you're fired."

Talk about shocking.

"You're my mom," I say. "You can't fire me."

She raises an eyebrow, a challenge.

"It's mean," I say, trying again. "You can't fire me because it's mean."

"You should have thought of that before you behaved the way you did."

"And . . . Taylor?" I say. Taylor wouldn't have done any of this if I hadn't roped her into it. "Please don't fire her, too."

Mom glances over at Taylor, who's still, like, hard at work while this is going on. "Taylor has nothing to worry about," she says. "*You*, though. You should get home."

"Okay," I pout. She is really not changing her mind. "I'll get my stuff."

"And Dani," she says as I have my back turned, "you're grounded, too."

"No!" I say-shout. "You can't ground me—this weekend is the Midnight Movie."

"You can't go to the movie. That's what grounding means."

"You've never grounded me before. . . ."

She thinks for a moment. "That's true. I never needed to."

"So?" I say.

"So . . . welcome to your first grounding."

I don't put up a fight after that. I just head out, and not even Taylor makes a move to stop me. This is what you get when you say you're only trying to help: You get fired, you get grounded, you get told you're selfish, told you're creepy, told to go away.

And then there are the big, fat liars of the world like Jackson, walking free.

I'm home, on my computer in my bedroom (because I may be grounded, but my mom's still at work and hasn't taken away the Internet yet) when I get my chance.

Nichole accepted my friend request. She also sent me a message:

Don't think this means anything.

And btw you still can't use my bathtub when you stay here.

Nichole and that stupid tub. That's the first thing I'm going to do next time I'm at my dad's house: take a long, hot, lavender-scented bubble bath. I'm going to soak in that tub until all the bubbles go flat and I turn into a lavender-smelling prune.

But I try to forget all about the bath because I made Nichole my friend online for a reason. Bella is easy to find—Nichole has one friend named Bella, a girl called Bella B. Her photo is a picture of two feet in polka-dot socks. This time, the spots are turquoise. I can't see Bella B.'s page unless I add her as a friend and I'm not *that* reckless, but I can see the comments she's left for Nichole.

can't come over 2nite i'm seeing my bf! ;) she says the night I spotted her at the playground.

jackson's coming by 2day :D . . . c u 2morrow? 8) she says a day I didn't even know Jackson skipped town.

Just yesterday, Bella B. says: *i'm sad, n. come cheer me up. j too busy 2 come over this saturday. he works all the time :(:(:(:(:(:(:(:(:(:(:(:(:(*

I can't find Jackson online, but no matter. From my sleuthing I've discovered a few things about the mysterious Bella B. For one, she's obviously in love with polka dots. She's also very partial to emoticons.

But most troubling is what she called Jackson: her bf. This girl actually thinks Jackson is her boyfriend. And, at the same time, Elissa thinks he's *her* boyfriend. So who's the Other Woman in this situation? Which one is the femme fatale?

I decide to write Nichole back. What comes out is this:

I don't even want to use that ugly tub. You're just as evil as your mom, imho. I wish my dad never gave her that ring.

Tell your friend Bella if she wants to know why Jackson can't see her Saturday, she should check the Shanosha paper for the Midnight Movie, Sat. night. His REAL GF will be there.

Then, before I even read it back, I hit send.

I may not be there on Saturday, but *this is not about me*—no matter what Taylor or Austin or Mom may think. Whatever stupid movie fantasies I had flickering in my head about Jackson and me (untold, unspoken things like a propeller plane rising into a black-and-white starry night with us on it, like him waiting till I'm in high school to say he forgot one thing, and I say *What*, and he says, *You*) are cutting to black now. Fade out on all that. I'm done. This is about Jackson getting what he deserves before it's too late. This is justice, or revenge, or something I just made up that's way better. This is the real movie. The rest was only the previews.

It's only after dinner, late at night when I'm in bed, unable to sleep because I'm wallowing in my grounding, that I think about what I just did.

Maybe Elissa won't want to find out this way.

Maybe Bella is just as nice as Elissa even though she's friends with awful tub-hogging Nichole. Maybe Bella works at the ice-cream shop on the other side of the river and babysits kids the way Elissa babysat for me.

But you can't stop a message once you've sent it.

And, still, there's this small part of me that's hoping nothing will come of it. That hopes Nichole will delete the message before even reading it because she made it clear she has no interest in knowing me anyway. There's a part of me that wonders if I did the right thing and wishes, you know, just for a second before I fall asleep, if there's some way I could maybe take it back.

18

You Call This a Midnight Movie?

T*he first frame is pitch-black.* It's the kind of black that's so black it's probably made out of every single color you can think of. It's a black that has nothing and everything in it at the same time. Like a room crammed too full of rainbow jimmies.

You blink. You wonder if the movie's even started yet. But it has. You can hear the sound, crackling, the dinosaur soundtrack spitting and hissing as it spools forward inch by agonizing inch. Until, at last, you hear something you understand. It's a word, coming up through the static. It's— It's— It happens to sound a lot like your name.

My name, actually.

What movie did I just walk into, and who's saying my name?

"Dani!"

That's when I open my eyes and realize I'm not in a movie theater after all. I'm at home, in my room, lights off, a sheet pulled over my head.

Grounded.

Someone is outside my window, calling up to me from the lawn below. I kick off the sheet and peek at the clock: It's Saturday, way past nine o'clock at night. Which means the Midnight Movie—you know, the one my mom won't let me go to?—starts soon. I stomp over to the window, dragging the sheet like a slack, useless cape, and look out to find Austin and Taylor. They're outside, waving at me with abandon.

"What are you guys doing here?" I hiss down at them. This is my first time being grounded, so my mom may not be too familiar with the rules, but I don't think entertaining guests on the lawn below your bedroom window would count as punishment.

Austin mumbles something from behind his hand. It sounds like *"Shhh-mu-bup."*

"What?" I whisper.

"Shhh-mu-bup," he repeats.

I never thought I'd say this, but I almost wish he had the walkie-talkies. Taylor tries to sign out the meaning with her hands. It's a good thing she's never gone out for cheerleading because her arms are all over the place, and I can't tell if she's motioning that they just dug up a grave or that it's okay to make a left turn.

It's so fitting that I'm grounded from my cell phone and can't call them—not that my phone works in here anyway. It's like I'm trapped in the Stone Age, or in 1992—it doesn't matter when, just before cell phones were invented. How did people communicate way back a long time ago before they could even text?

Letters. They wrote each other letters. Like, on paper.

I get out a notebook from last year's math class, find a blank page, and write: I DON'T UNDERSTAND A WORD YOU'RE SAYING!

I've been told I have perfect handwriting—when I write in all capital letters, it looks like a movie marquee.

Down below, Taylor rummages in her bag and pulls out—no joke—a notebook. Does she carry pen and paper with her everywhere she goes now? Guess so.

She writes: SHE SHOWED UP! YOU HAVE TO COME!

WHO, BELLA??????????? I scribble, my handwriting not so cinematic now.

Taylor and Austin nod wildly.

And that's how I know my plan to catch Jackson has gone on without me. Nichole got my message and told Bella. And Bella's at the Little Art right now, where everyone in town—Elissa included—will see her.

I make what's known as a split-second decision. It's like this: I can (1) stay in bed and practice wallowing or (2) risk double-grounding and go see what happens.

"I'm coming down!" I hiss. Now zoom out the camera and give me some room here, because my mom will catch me for sure if I use the stairs.

I get dressed, fast. I shove a few stuffed animals in my bed—yes, I have a few stuffed animals somewhere I'm not going to say, don't judge. I know what I'm doing because I've seen the stuffed-animal method in movies. Or was it TV?

Maybe it's something hormonal that blooms in you when you become a teenager (even when nobody treats you like one). Escaping from being grounded becomes a survival skill. Because, to me, it comes naturally.

I climb out my window to the roof. This might sound dangerous, like I've gone off the rails and leaped into a spy movie. But once I admit that this part of the roof connects to a low overhang on top of the garden shed, no taller than the rakes we keep in it, I might seem a smidge less brave than I'm making myself out to be. Also, there's a wall of wooden lattice to climb down, like a ladder made just for me, so escaping off the rooftop isn't as hard as it may sound.

I guess someone forgot to tell Austin.

He has one leg up on the lattice. He's reaching for me like I'm some helpless girl who needs a hand getting down.

"Get out of the way," I tell him.

"I'm helping," he whispers.

"You're not," I say. I kick out with my leg, seeking the next foothold, but Austin's hand is in the way.

"Ow!" he says while at the same time I say, "Move!" while at the same time I hear Taylor say, "Guys, watch out!" And then there's this sickening little crunch.

"Ow ow ow ow ow ow," Austin whimpers, and falls, and since it's nighttime it seems like he falls way farther than the two feet between here and the lawn. It sounds like he drops off the top of a very tall building and lands, with a horrible crack, far down below where I can't even see.

I scramble to the ground just as Taylor rushes over to him. He's sprawled on his back, holding his left arm. I have visions—blood and gore. Snapped bones. Phone calls to each of our moms.

"Are you okay?" I ask him. "Did you get hurt? Austin, say something!"

"I'm fine," he says at last. "I think I just landed on a twig."

Sure enough, when he rolls over there's a broken stick beneath him.

"You shouldn't have tried to climb up. I was fine without you," I tell him.

"I was trying to help!"

"You were making it worse!"

"Shhhh!" Taylor says. She points at the house. A light has come on in the kitchen on the first floor. We huddle together on the grass, keeping as quiet and still as we can. My mom can be seen crossing the room. She steps closer until she's right in front of the window facing the lawn. She stands there, and I'm positive she can see us out here, a makeshift pyramid of fear near her geraniums, but then she just looks down. She keeps her eyes lowered, her arms and shoulders moving, in the midst of doing something.

"She doesn't see us, does she see us?" Taylor says.

In the window, my mom reaches up and puts something aside: a blue mug.

"She's just doing dishes," I say, sighing with relief. And with that, we step out of our pyramid and head for the driveway and the road into town. We begin to run as fast as we can. The only problem is Austin, who's lagging.

I stop, waiting for him to catch up. "What's wrong? Did you break your legs or something?"

But when he runs up, his legs seem perfectly fine. Then I see, under a streetlight, how he's still cradling his left arm.

"My wrist sort of hurts," he admits.

Taylor takes a moment, inspecting it with her flashlight. "It's swollen," she says. "What should we do?" she asks, looking straight at me.

We're about four blocks from the Little Art—and the Midnight Movie, the one starring Rita Hayworth, is about to begin. Inside that theater we will find Jackson and his girlfriend, Elissa, not to mention his other girlfriend, Bella. Worlds are already colliding in the darkness just blocks from where we're standing and here we are hesitating on the sidewalk. Well, girlfriends are colliding, anyway, and we're so close.

I guess I took too long to answer because Austin answers for me. "Let's just go," he says, with a glance at me. "The movie's starting."

So that's how I find myself stepping into Theater 1 at close to 10:15 on a Saturday night when I'm supposed to be home grounded. I slip into the back row and cast my eyes out over the darkened theater, searching for Elissa and then for Bella, but not finding either in the rows and rows of seats.

Jackson was hoping his Midnight Movies would draw a crowd—he planned on getting a take from the box office for his car fund. And, actually, there are dozens of people here, dozens and dozens. I can imagine Jackson sitting up there on his throne in the projection booth, looking out over the crowd and feeling like a rock star. He made this happen. He'll have his car in no time.

It's like whatever Jackson wants, Jackson gets. Everything—and anyone.

The picture comes up and a hush falls over the audience. No one here has any idea what's about to happen—and I don't just mean the movie.

In *The Lady from Shanghai*, Rita Hayworth has gone blond. I almost don't recognize her. Then I remember how it happened. Supposedly the guy making the movie—Orson Welles, her husband at the time—talked her into changing her hair for the character, bleaching it platinum blond and cutting it short. When she did, people freaked. The Rita Hayworth they knew and loved had changed—and she hadn't asked permission.

They thought she was one thing, and how dare she go and become something else.

It makes me wonder how people see *me*. Maybe they think I'm the mean one, the selfish one. The one who told Bella to come here. The one who wants to hurt Elissa by forcing her to face the truth. The one who can't be with Jackson so she wants no one to have him—but that's wrong, and not who I am, not at all. I just don't know how to prove otherwise.

Taylor elbows me as if she can hear my thoughts and wants to get her vote in. On-screen, Rita Hayworth is gazing out at the audience, making it so no one can look away, not the guy she wants to like her in the movie, and not me.

"What?" I whisper.

"Look," says Taylor.

"I *know*," I breathe. "She's perfect, no matter what color her hair is."

"Huh?" Taylor says. She's not pointing at the glamorous

movie star, she's pointing at the left-hand side of the theater. With the reflection of light casting off Rita Hayworth's bright blond hair, we can see a little better. And it looks like Taylor's found Elissa. She's right there, sitting in a row with a group of friends.

But Taylor's not done yet. "Look," she insists. Now she's pointing at the other side of the theater, the right-hand side, opposite of where Elissa is sitting.

In those seats, a few girls can be made out in the darkness. I recognize one as Nichole. And the other, the one sitting in the aisle? It's Bella. I see her only in profile, the flip of her hair, the line of her nose and lips.

She's here.

19

The Femme Fatale, Take Two

C*all it detective smarts,* call it plain old intuition, but I have a bad feeling.

I can picture the final scene and it sends shivers all up and down my spine: Bella will be with Jackson in one part of the theater, and Elissa will be with Jackson in another part of the theater. He'll be running back and forth, lying to them both. The girls won't ever be in the same place at the same time, so they'll never know the truth. Jackson will get away with this the way people in movies can get away with murder.

Or—what's worse?—Jackson will be with Bella in the lobby. They won't be getting popcorn. And, right then, Elissa will come out and see them together, and her heart will break in pieces all over the black-painted floor, and it won't look like a universe of stars in the night sky but like a heart that got broken, which I don't think even looks like anything, and I'll never be able to eat popcorn again.

I can't let it happen. Not to Elissa, no matter that she's mad at me and got me in trouble with my mom. "I'm going to tell her," I say. I climb over Taylor so I can slip out into the aisle.

Only, someone's holding me back. Literally. Taylor has a good grip on my sleeve and is tugging at me to keep me from escaping into the aisle. She pulls me down into a seat. "You can't just go down there and tell Elissa," she says.

"Why not?"

"In front of her friends? In the middle of the movie? It'll just make things worse."

"Wouldn't you want someone to tell you?"

"I don't know," she says, after thinking about it. "Maybe I'd be too embarrassed."

"But—" I stop talking when someone in the next row

shushes me. Maybe Taylor's right. Maybe I should wait for the right moment. Whenever that is.

On screen, Rita Hayworth is being her usual incredible self, except the movie's making it seem like we're not supposed to trust her. Come to think of it, I'm beginning to wonder about this movie, about why Jackson chose it.

The music is filled with loud horns and wicked violins. We focus on a room surrounded on all sides by mirrors, a carnival fun house. Then the music cuts out and Rita Hayworth's standing in the dark with a white-hot flashlight in her hand. In the mirror maze there are now four Rita Hayworths, the blaze of her eyes multiplied out into forever. She steps closer, and in all the many mirrors she takes one step closer more times than you can count.

"We could have run off together," Rita Hayworth says to her secret boyfriend. Her voice is flat. Her eyes betray nothing. She loves no one, not even herself.

Then some other guy steps onto the screen—her husband. The mirrors show three of him, six, eight, more. She looks scared now, caught.

He tells her she'd better not fire that gun she's holding. "With all these mirrors, it's difficult to tell," he says. "You *are* aiming at me, aren't you?"

Shots ring out, and glass shatters and is reflected shattering and shattering.

That's the movie.

But then I lose sight of the movie because right here in the theater someone stands up. A girl. Light bounces off the screen and makes her glow around the edges like an approaching eclipse. I can't make out her face, but I don't need to see the face to know who it is. She's Bella, the girl who thinks she's Jackson's girlfriend. And she's heading for the projection booth.

Elissa—who also thinks she's Jackson's girlfriend—is now coming up the other aisle, the aisle on my side. Which means she's close enough for me to do something. Distract her. Warn her, even. I reach out my arm as she passes and my fingertips graze something—her elbow, I think. But whatever it was I'll never know because what my fingers catch is air.

Elissa goes to the door on her side of the projection booth and knocks. In the other aisle, Bella walks to the door on her side. But she doesn't knock, she just goes on in.

"It's happening," Taylor whispers to me like I can't see with my own two eyes.

Sitting on the other side of Taylor, Austin actually has his hands over his eyes like we're watching a horror movie.

And what do I feel, while Elissa knocks again on the door and is about to go in, while Bella's in there already, while the movie rolls and the audience takes it in, while on-screen Rita Hayworth isn't the Rita Hayworth I thought I knew?

I feel nothing at first. Like I'm separate from all of it. Like it's nothing to do with me—Jackson and Bella and Elissa—it's to do with them.

Then again, it's because of me that Bella knows about the Midnight Movie. So I'm not as separate as I'd like to think.

Elissa stops knocking but doesn't go away. She opens the door and walks in.

Voices can be heard, voices that have nothing to do with the movie. I can't even pay attention to Rita Hayworth. I turn around.

It's hard to make out what they're saying. I want to follow Austin's lead and cover my ears. I want to crawl under the seat and disappear.

Suddenly the picture freezes. The speakers squeak to a halt. There are protests from the audience, people turning around in their seats to see what's up.

Now would be a good time to slip out of the theater and go back home before my mom knows I snuck out.

Taylor and I meet eyes. Before this week, I would have said we're definitely not friends anymore, definitely. I would have said we're practically strangers. A whole school year has gone by, which is like fifty years when you're in junior high. Only thing is, I'm looking into her eyes and I know exactly what she's thinking. Just as you would if you were looking at your best friend.

She's thinking we need to get out of here. Like, now.

And I bet she knows what I'm thinking too. She knows how awful I feel. She knows I think this is my fault.

She looks at me and her eyes say it's not my fault, not entirely. But, either way, her eyes say, *We really need to go.*

My eyes say, *Okay.*

Her eyes say, *Then move!*

I'm the one closest to an aisle, and the exit. I head for the door, but just before I reach it the house lights come on. Austin's at the switch, turning on the lights so everyone can see. Next I hear someone yelling. At me.

"You!" I hear. She's all up in my face before I even get out into the lobby.

Hey, everyone, meet Nichole. My dad's marrying her mom, so we're almost related.

"You little brat," she says.

I don't say anything back. There's something about Nichole that makes my tongue go limp, makes me forget I even have one and wonder if I've gone and swallowed it. She just brings out the tongue-swallowing tendencies in me.

Nichole has her hands on her hips, elbows up and out. Her straightened blond hair whips all around her like a sharp, pointed sandstorm.

"You think this is funny, don't you?" she blasts at me. She means the big scene in the projection booth. The one everyone in the theater couldn't help but witness.

"No," I squeak in protest.

"You told us to come here," Nichole says. "You totally set this up."

"No," I protest again—though I did, didn't I? I set this all up.

"Oh and, *by the way*, I told my mom what you said about her. Your dad freaked." She gives an evil grin.

Elissa peeks out of the projection booth. I'm standing just beside it, inches away. She's heard everything. "You set this up?" she asks me quietly.

My eyes say all.

"You knew and you didn't tell me?" she says, her voice cracking.

Someone could come to my defense here. Someone like Taylor, though she's still down in the aisle, and I guess it's not exactly fair of me to expect her to speak up for me. To use her only when I need her, like I guess I've done before.

"I tried," I tell Elissa. "Remember?"

"Oh," she says, remembering when I chased her in the rain, "that." She looks horribly sad. Or embarrassed. I can't tell the difference.

It's okay—Elissa knows I had her back, she's got to—but then someone has to ruin it. "She really was going to tell you," Austin says. Now he's standing up near the projection booth too. "She was going to show you the picture."

I widen my eyes like stop signs: *Shut it! Do not mention the picture!*

"There really is a picture?" Elissa says in a low voice.

"You took a *picture*?" Bella says. I guess she's here to confront me too.

Nichole just says, "You little brat." It's become, like, her nickname for me.

Jackson has no words—he's just standing in the booth staring me down.

Actually everyone's staring me down—I can see the audience

looking up the aisle at me, like I'm the movie people came out to see.

Finally Jackson speaks. "D," he says, "I knew you were at the playground that night, no matter what Austin said. So you got a picture. Let's see it."

"I want to see it," Elissa says, not too convincingly, and then Bella adds, "Yeah, show it," and even Nichole, who has nothing whatsoever to do with this and should really just stay out of it, adds, "Yeah."

So I reach into my pocket to dig out my cell phone and show them the incriminating picture at the seesaws. My phone isn't there, so I try the pocket on the other side of my pants. I try my back pocket. I stop trying—I've run out of pockets.

Then, of course, I remember. "I don't have my phone," I say. "I'm grounded and my mom took it."

"Then what are you doing here," Nichole says, "if you're grounded?"

She has no right to act like a big sister, and I'm about to call her on it, except she sort of has a point. "I guess I can't show anyone the picture," I say.

Jackson doesn't respond.

"Never mind," Elissa says. "It doesn't matter. I think we

should break up." She's looking down at the floor when she says it, but we all know who she's talking to.

"Yeah, Jackson, we're done," Bella shoots out. With all the panic going on, all the stopping of movies and ruining Rita Hayworth's big scene, I hadn't even really thought of the fact that the lights are now on, and I can see Bella. The femme fatale is standing right here in front of me. In full color. For the first time.

The only images I had of her before were pieces:

A pair of legs in polka-dot tights.

A silhouette on the seesaws.

Two feet in a photo online.

The outline of her face in the dark.

An eclipse sneaking up the aisle.

Now that I can see her, she's pretty, sure. What did you expect? And yet . . . if she's supposed to be the femme fatale, I don't see it. She looks like some girl in high school. Some girl who seems really upset.

So if Bella's not the femme fatale in this situation, and Elissa's not the femme fatale, then I guess one doesn't exist. I hadn't considered that before. Unless it's supposed to be me, because of how I've acted and what I've done?

While I'm trying to make sense of this, Jackson has been trying to do something of his own: make excuses. I take it he's waiting to see which one will stick.

"It's just, you know, we never said exclusive," he's telling Elissa. Or is it Bella. It doesn't matter, because neither of them seems interested.

"Save it," Elissa says. She starts for the exit.

I guess the night's drama is about over. But then the door to the lobby comes open and a whole new round of drama storms in. My mom.

"Danielle," is all she says. That's all she has to say.

Ms. Greenway is right behind her. "I called her," she says. "I happen to know you're grounded, Danielle."

The moment is beyond awkward for me, but then I see the look on my mom's face as she notices the girl standing near me, Nichole. By the way she's staring at her, I know she knows who Nichole is. Nichole also studies her but without the usual smirk.

Suddenly, thankfully, something catches my mom's attention. It's Austin—only, I don't think he means to be the diversion. He's cradling his wrist, groaning under his breath.

"Austin," my mom says, "what's wrong with your arm?"

His mom, Ms. Greenway, reaches out to check it and before her finger even grazes his skin he yelps in pain. It can't be *that* bad . . . can it?

"What happened?" his mom asks.

"I fell on it," he says.

"How?" his mom says. "When?"

"On the stairs?" he lies. "Before?" Vague is good, Austin, very good. Though I can't help wondering why he doesn't just out me as the person who stomped on his hand and knocked him off the roof. . . .

Taylor doesn't open her mouth to dispute any of this.

Everyone's like, *Oh, poor Austin, you tripped and fell on your own wrist.*

All eyes are on Austin now. Everyone surrounds him. Even Nichole.

I hear a chorus of "Austin, are you okay?" "Wow, it's really swelling up." "Do you think it's broken?" And I catch Austin's eye and hold it for one long second. You could say he broke his wrist for me.

You could.

"Maybe we should go to the ER?" he says to his mom.

It's at this point that I notice Jackson looking at me, like he wants a defender or something. An apologist. Like he thinks I'll still hang around and make up excuses to ask him about his favorite femme fatale after what he's done.

Rita Hayworth wouldn't care for a guy like Jackson. No girl who knows what she's worth ever would.

I turn away from him, to the dark movie screen. I don't need to see Rita Hayworth up there to know what to do.

"Can you start the movie up again or what?" someone in the audience shouts.

We look at him in shock like we'd forgotten we're standing in a theater, where people go, you know, to see movies. Jackson leaps to start up the projector, before anyone can ask for their money back. He may have been betrayed by me, and lost both his girlfriends, but he's still betting on that car. No one here is getting a refund.

20

Not You Too, Rita Hayworth

D*ays have passed,* days and nights, and I still don't know how *The Lady from Shanghai* ends. I'm not allowed out to the movies, and I don't see anyone airlifting the movie screen over here to me. So I'm out on my rooftop as usual. Only, I'm not pretending to get a tan or waiting for a phone call. I'm doing what any grounded almost-fourteen-year-old would do if forced to stay home during summer vacation.

Sulking.

Sulking is an art. I learned it from my brother, Casey, who

didn't need words—he could do it just by the way he breathed. He'd be sitting at dinner and let out this sigh of air—a drawn-out, discontented hiss. He'd act like the whole world was against him, even that night's leftover spaghetti.

And once my dad said he was moving out, Casey took it to the next level. When Mom told him to go help Dad move the tools out of the garage, Casey let everyone know what he thought of the tools—and Dad for taking them—and Mom for letting Dad take them—by dropping them in the geraniums so Dad would have to lug them to his new house all covered in dirt. Come to think of it, how I'm the one home grounded and Casey's away at camp is beyond me.

So I'm sulking up on the roof, but there's no point sighing my discontent or dropping anything in the geraniums because, for one, Mom hasn't really been keeping up with the gardening, but also because no one would see. Mom is still at work.

Just when I set my sulk out on the horizon—aiming it at the Catskill Mountains, the blue lumps poking up through the trees—a car pulls into the driveway. Elissa's at the wheel. She steps out and calls, "Can I come up?"

I'm glad she's here—though I haven't seen her since the

Midnight Movie and I'm nervous about it. Still, when you're sulking, it's best to keep a face of stone. So I tell her, "If you want to," and I point her to the ladder of lattice that's a straight climb up from the lawn. Elissa shakes her head and goes inside the house so she can climb out through my bedroom window instead. Maybe she heard how Austin really got that sprained wrist.

She says, "Your mom told me you'd probably be up here."

"My mom? Why, did you call her again or something?"

She keeps her eyes trained on the faraway mountains. "Actually . . . this time, she, uh, called me and asked me to come over tonight."

I take a turn staring at the faraway mountains. It's funny how the mountains can seem so distant when you're actually sitting in them. That's when it hits me. My mom asked her to come over.

"Is my mom *paying* you to be here?" I blurt out.

The mountains are the most fascinating things Elissa has ever seen—at least, that's what you'd think by the way she's staring at them.

"Like a babysitter?" I say.

Elissa breaks her gaze, finally. "Yeah."

A babysitter. At my age. Imagine the injustice.

"But I wanted to come," Elissa's quick to say. "And your mom's working late tonight to get the paper out, and—"

"And she doesn't trust me to stay home at night by myself."

Elissa shrugs. "That's what you get when you sneak out."

"Karma," I say in agreement. I can't be mad at Mom—no matter how lame it makes me feel knowing she had to *pay* someone to hang out with me. The night I got in trouble, the night she met Nichole, she said she thought Nichole seemed sweet. How nice I'll have a sister soon, she said. (Yes, she uttered the S-word, she really and truly did.)

She said it in this weird way, all cheerful and fake like there were other unspoken words beneath the words on top, and I'd have to dig under them to hear what she really meant. It felt like a sundae covered in chocolate coating that reveals, when poked with a spoon, something only a stodgy old person would eat, like butter pecan. So I knew that by saying Nichole seemed sweet my mom was really saying Cheryl was sweet, and by that she was saying if I loved Cheryl so much why didn't I just move in?

I could see the butter pecan and I wasn't having it. "She's not sweet," I told my mom. "She's awful." And, that same night,

I made a symbolic gesture. I deleted Nichole from my friends online—that one's for you, Mom. (Not that I didn't have a huge smile on my face during the process, though.)

Elissa's back to staring out at the mountains, and even though she's getting paid to do it, I guess I should say something. Like, *I'm sorry.* . . . Is that enough?

She surprises me by speaking first. "So I saw it. I thought you'd want to know."

She saw it . . . wait, she saw *it*? It, as in the photo? "When?" I say.

"The other night," she says vaguely.

"Who showed you?" Someone must have got on my phone to copy the photo. Someone stole it. Some nosy person thought they'd—

"Jackson," she says, "obviously."

I can't figure out how he got a hold of it.

I thought about erasing the picture, deleting it from memory like it never existed. But I had to see it first. I remember pointing my phone at the seesaws, snapping the photo, then running for my life. What I don't remember is taking a look at what I shot.

And now that I have, I know you wouldn't necessarily get

that it's a picture of Jackson and Bella. You wouldn't see see-saws, or two people on them, or anything recognizable as a physical object taking up space in the actual world. The picture looks like two snowmen doing the hula during an earthquake. If you squint.

"You look so upset!" Elissa says. "I'll tell you the end if you want. Rita Hayworth turns out to be the bad guy. Then she dies. Spoiler. Sorry."

"What?"

"*The Lady from Shanghai*," she says. "What did you think I was talking about?"

"The picture," I say. "The picture I took. Of Jackson?"

I see my cell phone, propped up on the rooftop between two shingles in the one micrometer of a spot where it gets decent reception. I want to throw it off the roof, see how far it'll fly—maybe I can aim it at the farthest peak of the farthest mountain.

"Oh no," Elissa says. "I actually really don't want to see the picture. Like, ever."

"I'm sorry," I say. I should probably say it a thousand times more. I'm thinking I may need to walk around town wearing a sign that says it. SORRY SORRY SORRY SORRY SORRY SORRY until people think I'm pitiful enough to forgive me.

"It's okay," Elissa says. "You were just looking out for me." She pauses. "Right?"

"Right. That's what I was trying to do. . . ."

"It's not that you were jealous," she says, watching me carefully.

"No," I say. "It's not."

She makes a face at the phone. "Just don't ever show me that picture."

"Never," I say. "'Cause I'm going to delete it." I grab the phone and open the image. It doesn't matter that you can't decipher anything from it, that's not the point. The point is that it exists. And once I hit erase it doesn't exist anymore. Easy as that. Like it never happened. Done.

Seeing Elissa's face, I wish it was like it never happened. I guess you can't erase that it did.

"So," I say, "*The Lady from Shanghai*. How'd you know I haven't seen the end?"

"Your mom said you can't stop talking about it." She smiles. "And I told her you wouldn't like the end, so maybe it's better that you didn't see it."

"Rita Hayworth, the bad guy? I don't believe it."

"Believe it!"

I shake my head to make it go away. I mean, if Rita Hayworth isn't perfect, then, tell me, who is?

Speaking of what's not perfect, Elissa's talking about something else. Something I could spend eternity not thinking about, or talking about, even if it meant imprisonment on this rooftop with only the mountains for company for the rest of my life.

"Things happen, things you can't change. It's hard at first, but then you get used to them, you know," Elissa's saying.

She's trying so hard, but all I'll give her is a shrug. Just the one.

"Like with me and Jackson," she says. "Maybe it won't hurt so much by . . . October."

She said the word "October." My mom must have told her about the wedding.

"Like, maybe by then I'll be used to it." My mom totally told her.

So I up and say it. "What, like Cheryl marrying my dad? I'll get used to it?"

"Eventually," Elissa says, "probably."

I'll believe *that* when I see it.

"Yeah, who knows," Elissa says. "Maybe by October you'll be really close with Nichole and you two'll be bridesmaids at your dad's wedding or whatever."

I clutch my throat, doing a dramatic rendition of a gag.

"Maybe by then your mom'll be all totally okay again, and the divorce will be the best thing that could have happened."

"Yeah," I say, scoffing. "And maybe I'll grow up to be a movie star like Rita Hayworth."

"Maybe by then I'll have a new boyfriend, too," Elissa continues. And this stops me, and I don't even pretend to gag.

"Maybe before that," she continues. And she actually smiles. Because it turns out—it's a good thing I'm sitting down—that she already likes someone new.

"But you and Jackson—" I say. "You just— I mean, you just broke up."

She shrugs. "Like I said, things happen."

Of course I have to ask. "Who is it?"

"Ryan?" she says. "You know Ryan . . . he works at the tube-rental place."

I wrinkle my nose. "I hate tubing. I have no idea who Ryan is."

"You'll like Ryan."

And I guess I'll have to. Because any boyfriend of Elissa's is a friend of mine, right? But if I lose my tube and get shot down the rapids tubeless and contract river poisoning and practically almost drown, I might not like him for long.

"Hey." Elissa kicks my foot. "Jackson's leaving town at the end of the month, so, yeah, I'm steaming mad at the jerk for not telling me he had that girlfriend back home, and it really hurt, it really did. But—" She pauses and looks like she's about to say something very deep but just says, "But oh well, right?"

"I guess," I say. Though two words I would not use to describe the drama this summer are "oh" and "well." If I'd been the one with Jackson, I don't know if I'd let it go so easily. I don't even want to let it go right now.

"You have to come tubing with me," she says, "so you can meet Ryan."

"Elissa, I seriously despise tubing."

"So do I," she says, "but you know how it is . . . to think you like someone, but all along you liked someone else. Or you should've. . . ." And here, if you can believe it, she grins. "Admit it," she says.

"Admit what?"

"You *know* what!"

Here I am wondering if we've been sitting in the theater watching two different movies when she tackles me. She lunges at me across the rooftop, claws out to tickle me into a confession, and I roll away from her, and one false move and we'll both tip off the roof and flatten what's left of my mom's geraniums.

"Careful!" I shriek. "Or we'll fall off like Austin!"

Elissa stops at the roof's edge and laughs. "So that's how he messed up his wrist. I knew you had something to do with it, even though he swore up and down you didn't."

I roll my eyes involuntarily. Austin. Though I admit I'm surprised he hasn't told on me and made me pay his medical bills yet.

"Speaking of Austin . . ." Elissa says.

"Speaking of Austin what?"

"Wow, you can really play dumb," she says, and lets out a long sigh. "You do know he has the hugest crush on you, right? Jackson was going to tell you, but I said it was old news because you knew already. You *did* know, didn't you?"

"Sure," I say, I'm not sure how convincingly. "I mean, I figured." So that's what Jackson was blackmailing Austin with that time I overheard them.

A faint reaction bubbles up inside my chest. Some weird cagey feeling like I caught some living thing in there, and now it's knocking around to get out. I push it back down. I'm not in any way excited about this. No. That can't be it. The last time I liked someone—even if I never, ever admitted it out loud to anyone—he turned out to be a sinister con artist bent on crushing hearts and making off with a new car the first chance he got.

Just then, mercifully, before I can put the feeling to words, we're interrupted. Saved, by a ringing phone.

My cell phone is perched between the shingles, picking up all five bars. That's the good news. The bad news is who's calling. The Caller ID glows with a single word: DAD.

"You should get that," Elissa says. She climbs through my bedroom window into the house, leaving me alone with the phone and no dead zone to make it stop ringing.

I pick up before it goes to voice mail. "Hi, Dad," I mutter.

"Hello, Danielle. Listen, your mother told me you're grounded. And I heard about what happened at the movie theater from your sister."

"Dad, that girl is not my sister. I've only met her twice in my life."

"That's true," he says. "She's not your sister—yet. But she will be." Then he pauses for so long that I check my phone to be sure the signal hasn't cut out. If he's waiting for me to say something about how excited I am to snag myself a whole new family with this marriage he may as well wait up for the Tooth Fairy. Because he'll get a quarter under his pillow before he gets any lovey-dovey stuff about Nichole from me.

He starts talking again and won't stop. He says he heard what I said about Cheryl. And she's the woman who's going to become his wife, and I have to show some respect.

He says I can't keep giving my mom such a hard time. I can't lie to her; I can't sneak out. Then he says he heard I deleted Nichole, and we're going to be family soon and I should never delete family. I think he just called to yell at me about the Internet. Can you believe this?

"Danielle, what do you have to say for yourself?" Dad says.

What I have to say, he won't want to hear. Sometimes the bad guy is a person you love. A person you can't just kick out of your life. And when the picture fades out and the movie ends, and the curtain goes down, and the audience leaves the theater, you're stuck in what's known as real life. That's where all the lights are on and the flawed people you're related to are saying lines you don't want to hear and there's no one to yell "Cut!" to make it stop.

So what I say is: "I can't believe Nichole told on me about that, it's so stupid."

"Maybe so," he says. "I'm far more concerned about you and your mom. It sounds like things are out of hand."

This catches my attention. I shoot up straight, all blood rising to my head.

"I'm beginning to wonder if you should move in with me."

There. He's said it.

"*No,*" I say.

"Danielle, if your mother can't control—"

"Please," I say, stopping him. "I want to keep living with Mom."

"That's not the way you've been acting. Sneaking out. Lying. Running away . . ."

"I never ran away, I was faking. Besides, I can't leave Mom. Not after you did."

This shuts him up.

"I'm staying here," I insist. "I'm not moving anywhere."

It's funny. When those words come out, I mean them more than I've ever meant anything. Shanosha, the little nowhere place I've wanted to scribble off the map and you'd never know the difference—it's where I want to be.

"Besides, I can't live with you," I tell him. "How can I ever trust you again, after what you did?" It's like I'm the parent now, talking to the kid.

"That's a good question, Danielle," Dad says at last. "A good question."

And? And no answer. So what about this one: "And why?" I ask. "Why'd you have to go be with someone else and leave Mom? Why?"

That one gets even less of an answer. It gets a silence on the other end of the phone so deep and so long I think he may have up and left me, too.

Because you can't help who you like, can you? But you sure can help how you go about it. You can try with all that's in you not to lie.

Finally he speaks. "We have a lot to work through, you and I," he says. "And you're right. Moving in with me isn't going to solve it. So, will you start behaving?"

"Yes," I say. For my mom's sake. And, yes, I mean it.

"All right," he says. "And I hope you've changed your mind about attending the wedding. . . ."

"Maybe," I say. "Maybe not."

He sighs. "We'll talk about it another time. In the meantime, could you please apologize to Nichole for deleting her? She won't want me to say it, but she's pretty upset."

"Okay," I tell him. I'm doing it again: lying. There is no way I'm apologizing to Nichole, not for anything. I can't be *completely* rehabilitated, not this fast.

Once my dad and I are done, I head downstairs to find Elissa doing a search-and-rescue mission through our freezer to see what we can possibly scavenge to make for dinner. Talking to her and my dad brings up all these questions.

Like, How do you know what's real and what's a lie?

Like, What's love, and what makes it start and what makes it fall flat?

Like, What happens when someone you thought was wonderful turns out to be not-so-great?

Like, What do I want for dinner? Because Elissa's here right now, asking.

There are no answers.

I do know the answer to this one, though: Do I want to stay here with my mom, even if that means I have to stay in Shanosha? Yes. Totally, unanimously yes.

Call me crazy, but here I am with absolutely no cell-phone reception, and I'm grounded for who knows how many more weeks, and there's nothing good in the fridge to eat, and yet this is the only place in the whole world where I want to be.

Picture that.

21

Why, Hello, Lana Turner

I *see his bike in the driveway before I see him.* The bike's propped up by the kickstand, but no one's nearby. I wonder how long it's been out there.

Then, as I watch from the living room, I see him step off the porch and return to his bike without even saying hi. What was the point of riding over here anyway?

"Austin!" I call out the window.

He whips around at the sound of his name. "Hey," he says, looking guilty. "I left you something. It's on the porch."

This is when I notice the cast on his left arm—it covers his hand and reaches up to his elbow. He sees me looking and says, "It doesn't hurt. Not too bad."

I head out for the porch to see what he left for me. On the doormat is a DVD, *The Postman Always Rings Twice*. The femme fatale is a blonde in a bright gold dress. She looks off into the distance, up and away, like she has a secret.

Slowly, Austin takes just one step toward me—like I might bite him. "That's Lana Turner," he says. "She was discovered at a soda fountain. She was cutting school and went out for a milkshake and someone from Hollywood saw her. The rest is history."

"Huh," I say, taking a closer look. "Rita Hayworth was a flamenco dancer. She started dancing when she was like six years old."

"Yeah," he says. "I heard about that."

"So why this movie? You don't think I'll like Lana Turner better than Rita Hayworth, do you? Because that would be impossible."

"Oh, I know. I just thought you'd want to see this week's Midnight Movie. . . . I figured you wouldn't be allowed to go."

I leave that without comment. He's right, you know: There's no way my mom will let me go, and I'm not sneaking out, not again. So the fact that he rode all the way out here to give me my very own advanced screening is . . . let's just say it's not the usual Austin Greenway brand of annoying I've gotten so used to.

It's even sort of nice.

"You want to watch it now?" he asks.

Maybe I'm not myself today. Maybe the long period of grounding has messed with my senses and now I can't tell right from wrong from plain stupid. Because I'm standing here on my front porch with Austin and I'm not in any hurry to leave. I'm almost considering letting him come in and watch the movie with me.

Then he ruins it by going, "Or not."

So I say, "I have to mow the lawn anyway."

"Right," he says. He mumbles bye and starts down the steps. Then he turns back. There's a curious look on his face when he does, all clear-eyed and blinking like he held his head underwater for longer than he thought he could stand and came up at last. "What did I ever do to you anyway?" he says, more forcefully than I expected.

It's not like he's picking a fight. It's more like he just really wants an answer.

"Nothing," I say. "You didn't do anything."

"So?"

My head is empty of comebacks. *So . . . you annoy me?* That's all I've got.

He's still waiting for an answer.

"I can't talk . . . the lawn," I say. Then I add—because it's the truth and if I want everyone else to tell me the truth I should make a go at telling some too, "Okay, maybe not *today*. But my mom said I have to mow the lawn sometime this week."

He's walking away now. He's down the steps. He's halfway to his bike before I get the courage to say it.

"Can I ask you something?" I blurt out. He turns around but doesn't say yes or no. Still, I take it as a yes. "Is it true? That you have like a crush on me or whatever?"

I can't believe I put that thought into words. He looks about as shocked as I feel. He walks back so he's standing at the bottom of the stairs and I'm standing at the top. There are only four steps between the porch and the ground and I can't decide if he's too close, with just the four steps between us, or too far.

Is there something wrong with me?

"I guess Jackson told you," he says.

"No. I don't think Jackson's talking to me. Elissa told me. I think she thought I already knew."

"So you didn't?"

I shake my head, but that's not really true, is it? So I stop shaking my head and let it hang there, like maybe. Like maybe I knew and didn't want to say. Maybe, okay?

"For how long?" I ask. I need some clarity. "Since when?"

"Since the fourth grade," Austin says. "Since when you broke your violin string during the recital and that girl got mad because you almost poked her in the eye and you went off into the wings and we had to finish the song without you."

"No," I say in disbelief.

"Since that time you spilled your milk on me in the caf and I had to wear a wet shirt to the pep rally."

"No way."

"Since you tripped outside the library and you freaked that everyone saw, but hardly anyone was there, and no one would've known, if you'd just stopped talking about it."

"That's a long time," I say. "And also? I sound like a total idiot." I brave a smile.

He returns the smile, but he doesn't say if I am or I'm not. An idiot.

"You used to be nicer," he says.

I don't say if I was or I wasn't.

"So," he says, "are you going to stop talking to me, now that you know?"

"No." I deny it.

"Are you going to be even meaner?"

"No." I deny it some more.

"Because I'm not like him, okay?"

"Him?" I say.

"Him," he says. I wait for him to say Jackson's name, to call me on my mortifying crush and how he's way too old for me and a loser besides, and I got played. How every girl who likes Jackson gets played. But instead he goes, "Like Bogie."

I crack a smile. He doesn't though. He's not finished.

"So?"

"So . . . what?"

He's waiting for something, I don't know what. Then I know. He wants, like, an actual answer. I can't just stand here on the porch being an enigma. Maybe in the movies when a guy tells a femme fatale he's madly in love with her, she can get away with batting her eyelashes a few times and smiling the faintest whisper of a smile that means whatever he wants it to mean, depending on how closely he's looking. A femme fatale can be an enigma all she wants. She can walk off into the sunset as one, dragging his heart along with her.

Me? If I bat my eyes it's only because I think I got an eyelash stuck inside. I'm standing on my porch, in the bright-hot sunlight with nowhere to hide, and if I look anything it's probably just really confused. Because I am.

"I never had a girlfriend before," Austin says. "I know my cousin sucked at it, but I'll be way better."

Whoa. I step back, away from the stairs. "I didn't say I was your girlfriend."

"Yeah, okay."

"I never said that."

"I said I know."

"Good. Just so we're clear."

"Uh-huh."

All the while we're having this exchange he's got a goofy smile on his face, one that gets bigger with each word I utter.

"Thanks for the movie," I say. I'm holding the DVD out before me like a shield.

"No problem. I'll see you around?"

I nod. "If my mom keeps me grounded, it might not be till September. In school."

"Okay," he says. He says it like he doesn't mind. Like he could wait that long if that's how long it takes—that he'll be back, in September, ready to continue this conversation.

And he leaves me standing here, walking off to retrieve his bike. He rides away toward town, steering with his good arm. I watch. There's his dark hair catching in the wind as he takes the turn, his shirt flapping out behind him, his legs pumping. That's all I do: I stand here on the porch and watch. And what about that small smile on my face, my private attempt at being an enigma? It's better I keep it to myself for now. You know, spend more time practicing in front of a mirror first.

Because the little smile's not so little. For once, I'm sure glad this isn't a movie. I wouldn't want any cameras trained on me to catch sight of this.

I've invited Taylor over Saturday night—we'll have our own Midnight Movie, right here in my living room, I tell her. Only if she's interested, I say. Only if she wants to. I figure she doesn't owe me anything after how I treated her, but she surprises me by actually showing up.

"How's the internship?" I ask. I don't even think I sound sarcastic.

"Good," she says. "How's the grounding?"

"Good."

"Austin told me what happened."

I turn five shades of purple.

"We don't have to talk about it if . . ." she starts, leaving it dangling.

"Yeah," I say, relieved. "How about let's not?"

We steer the conversation away from Austin and boys in general. I don't know what I'm doing with Taylor, if this means we're officially friends again, if we're trying to go back in time to how it used to be. Because you can't do that, you know, you can't go back in time and pretend like a whole year never happened. People change, more than just their hairstyles, like Taylor wears hers up now and I've got bangs. People grow up.

I always figured Taylor was at a standstill while I was the one moving up in the world. But Taylor's different now too. Maybe we moved up a ways together, and we didn't even know it.

So we're here in my living room and my mom's here too.

She's here because it's a Saturday night and she has nothing else to do, but I don't mind.

I've noticed some things about her: No sobs behind walls, no dead stares at inanimate objects and forgetting about dinner. Sure, it's been only a week or so and anything could happen between now and tomorrow, but I have a feeling she's getting better. She has no idea Dad wanted me to go live with him, and I'm not going to tell her. It's enough that I said I wouldn't go. What I'll do is stick around, you know—keep an eye on her like she's keeping an eye on me.

The Postman Always Rings Twice begins with the usual thunder of horns, practically vibrating the TV off its stand. Lana Turner is the star, the head credits tell us, plus some guy we don't care about named John Garfield. We munch on a bowl of popcorn that my mom made on the stove as the rest of the names scroll. Then the picture comes up.

A drifter stops at a coffee shop, looking for a job to tide him over until he moves on to the next town. The owner gets excited someone's interested, but when another customer is outside waiting at the gas pump he has to leave the drifter alone for a minute.

That's when *she* comes in.

First, we see her tube of lipstick. It rolls into the room ahead of her—she must've dropped it, maybe on purpose. The drifter sees it there on the floor and goes to pick it up. Then his eyes travel to the doorway, to where she stands, the owner's wife: the most beautiful woman you know he's ever seen in his whole measly existence.

Here's Taylor: "Wow, is that Lana Turner?"

Here's Mom: "That's her."

And here's Lana Turner, turning her gaze to the drifter, and to us, her audience—and as soon as she does you know why she was grabbed from the soda fountain and made into a big star. You know why she's the femme fatale. She's magnetic.

As we watch I can't help stealing glances at my mom. The light from the movie shines over the room, illuminating her for me. She has an odd look on her face, one I don't recognize at first. Her eyes are open wide and sparkling. Her mouth is turned up at the corners, effortlessly. No stress crinkles on her forehead. No tight jaw. Wait, now I remember. This is what she looks like when she's happy.

Movies can do that: make people forget everything that's bad about their lives, and bad about the world, even make them ignore the fact that they've already run out of popcorn. All that matters is what's on-screen, that world in black-and-white or bright color, the story that's got its hold on you. Movies really can make it better.

If this were a movie and the sun was going down on Shanosha, the femme fatale would have the last laugh, of course, walking off into the sunset with all her secrets.

Maybe there'd be two femmes fatales, a mom fatale and a girl fatale, and they'd wear matching hats and keep each other's secrets. Maybe they'd walk off hanging on to their mystery, never turning into the bad guy or the good guy or anyone other than themselves. No one would break their hearts. Maybe the mom fatale would tell the girl fatale that she's not grounded anymore and she doesn't have to keep mowing the lawn.

Or not.

Mom catches me staring and casts her eyes down at the empty bowl. "I'll make you girls more popcorn," she says, getting up off the couch.

"No, really, Mom, we're okay," I tell her.

"Shhh," she says with a smile. "Watch your movie. I'll be back."

"This is really good," Taylor whispers. "I like her."

"Who, Lana Turner?"

"Yeah. I don't know, maybe she'll be my favorite movie star. We'll see. . . ."

"She's no Rita Hayworth."

"But she's great. Like seriously great. Admit it."

I'm staying loyal to Rita Hayworth, but I can't deny the truth: "Yeah," I say. "She's amazing."

We turn back to the movie. That's when my phone begins to ring. There's my cell, perched on the arm of the love seat across the room, somehow snagging a signal out of the scattered few that exist on this mountain.

My cell rings, and rings. It could be Casey calling from soccer camp, but I already talked to him this week. It could be my dad—but I doubt he'd call me this late on a Saturday night. I don't know who else could be calling. Then it hits me.

It's Maya, it has to be, finally getting around to calling me back from Poughkeepsie. I've been waiting for her call for weeks.

"Aren't you going to see who it is?" Taylor asks.

"Nah," I say. I know it's going to stop ringing soon, and Maya might never call back, but Taylor and me, we're in the middle of a movie. The femme fatale is drawing us closer and the cameras are sweeping in and the shadows are dark and deep and I can't tear my eyes away. This is what's happening in my real life, right now, the one I'm living.

I don't want to miss a thing, so I don't answer the phone—I don't even blink.

Acknowledgments

I need to thank Simon Pulse for giving my first published novel, *Dani Noir,* a second chance at life in this newly updated version of the story as *Fade Out.* Thank you to Anica Mrose Rissi, who found the book and believed in it enough to make this happen, and Jennifer Klonsky, Michael Strother, Craig Adams, Jessica Handelman, and everyone else at Pulse. And thank you to my agent, Michael Bourret, for making all things possible, always.

Thank you to those who were there at the beginning with *Dani Noir,* including Kate Angelella, Paul Crichton, Bernadette Cruz, Molly McLeod, Lisa Vega and the rest of the Aladdin team, Marc Breslav, Molly O'Neill, Micol Ostow, Mark Rifkin, Courtney Summers, and Christine Lee Zilka. And to the Writers Room, where this book was written.

Special thanks to Erik Ryerson, Laurel Rose Purdy, and Joshua Suma. And to Arlene Seymour, the most supportive mother a writer could ever ask for.